JiGGY AND THE WiTCHFiNDER

MICHAEL LAWRENCE

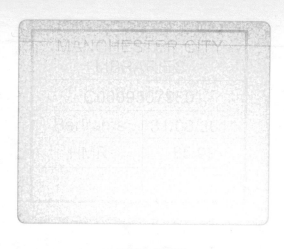

ORCHARD BOOKS
338 Euston Road, London NW1 3BH
Orchard Books Australia
Level 17/207 Kent Street, Sydney, NSW 2000

First published in the UK in 2011

ISBN 978 1 40830 805 9

A CIP catalogue record for this book is available from the British Library.

1 3 5 7 9 10 8 6 4 2

Orchard Books is a division of Hachette Children's Books, an Hachette UK company.

www.hachette.co.uk

'75% of our genetic make-up is the same as a pumpkin – 57% is the same as a cabbage.'

Anon, thehumangenome.co.uk

If you're new here, there are fifteen things you won't know about me apart from my name. Here are three of them.

1. I'm fantastically handsome.
2. I'm good at everything I do.
3. I lie a lot.

One thing I tell the absolute truth about is the stuff that goes into the school-type exercise books I hide under my bed with the fluff. I keep them there so my mother won't think she has a mad kid for a son. The old dear's bad enough already without that. Like, she has rules for everything. Even the time I spend brushing my teeth, would you believe.

'Five seconds, Jiggy,' she says. 'A record, even for you.'

'Wrong,' I say. 'A second and a half is my record.

I took my time because you were watching and getting all set to nit-pick, which you did.'

My mother is my harshest critic outside of Ranting Lane (my school). One of her favourite times of year is Parents' Evening, otherwise known as Swat the Kids Night because that's what it feels like to us. My mum looks forward to Swat the Kids Night because she can sit on a hard chair trashing me to my teachers and hearing them trash me back. Music to her sad old ears. Swat the Kids Night only occurs once a year, but that's once too often in my opinion. Pete and Angie's too. Pete Garrett and Angie Mint live across the road from me, with her mum and his dad. We're best buds. That's me, Pete and Ange, not me and his dad and her mum, though they're not so bad for Golden Oldies.

We were all on our way to the latest annual Swat. I sat in the back of our car with my baby sister Swoozie. Pete and Angie sat in the back of theirs with each other. When we reached the school car park we passengers got out – me carrying Swoozie – and went into the lobby to examine our fingernails while the dads drove round and round swearing about the shortage of parking spaces for non-disabled drivers. Parents and kids were swarming into the main hall where Swat Night was already well under way.

'You'd think they'd have something better to do, wouldn't you,' said Pete.

'I know I have,' said Angie.

When the dads eventually joined us, they and the mums charged into the hall, leaving the three of us (plus Swoozie, still in my arms) to follow. You may not be surprised to hear that we did not gallop eagerly after them. A few steps in we bumped into Eejit Atkins, my next-door neighbour and classmate. Atkins – never the brightest spark in the fireplace – was the only kid in sight who looked happy to be there.

'What's with the Edam grin, Eej?' I asked.

'I got a special award!' he said.

'You what?'

'I got a special award.'

'You? An award? A special one? What for?'

'One at a time, Jig,' said Ange. 'And slowly, this is Atkins.'

I repeated my questions, slowly, and gradually we got the answers. What had happened was that when Eejit and his mum got to Mr Dakin's table (Face-Ache Dakin's our form tutor) Dakin told Mrs Atkins that although her son's work, progress, concentration, interest and punctuality were about on a par with last time they'd met, he'd set such a good example on the class trip to the Edwardian Life Exhibition a few weeks ago that Dakin was giving him a special award entitled...

'Quietest Boy on the Bus?' I said, gaping at the Ranting Lane letterhead with some typing under it.

'Yer,' said Atkins proudly.

'I don't remember you on that trip,' said Pete.

'Nah, me neever,' said Atkins, still beaming.

'You weren't there,' said Angie.

'I weren't?' said Eejit.

'No, you snuck off the bus after they took the roll call. Went to the amusement arcade.'

'Oh yeah, that's right,' he said, finally clawing it all back. 'I got the jackpot on the Big Bonanza machine.'

The fact that he hadn't been on the bus didn't make him any less proud of the award, though – probably because he'd never had any kind of commendation from school before. His mum seemed pleased too. When the two of them left the hall, she walked with a fond hand on the little berk's shoulder.

I don't know how Parents' Evenings are arranged at other schools, but at Ranting Lane the kids have to book time with the teachers, and we're supposed to book at least five each. Sensible kids only book time with teachers they want their folks to meet, so five's stretching it for some of us. Sure is for me. My main two were Mrs Gamble and Mr Lubelski, who take us for English and Art, in that order. They're the only subjects I'm any good at. I'd also booked Religious Studies to annoy my dad, and Science because I was so short of options. I'd been tempted to book fitness supremo Mr Rice, but I couldn't do it in the end. I obviously wasn't the only one. While parents and kids lined up to see other teachers all around the hall Mr Rice, in his moron-red tracksuit, was running slowly on the spot beside his non-existent queue. Maybe he hoped running on the spot would drum up custom from stragglers who had no one better to see.

'Keep it up, sir, you'll get there in the end,' I said as we shuffled by.

'I haven't got you down on my list, McCue!' he shouted. Rice always shouts, though he was toning it down a bit tonight, probably because there were grown-ups about and this wasn't the sports field or the gym.

'That's because I still have half a brain,' I muttered.

As we hadn't arranged to see the same teachers at the same time, Angie and Pete went to find their parents while Swoozie and I went in search of ours. 'I don't want to depress you, Swooze,' I whispered as we shoved our way through the crowd, 'but in the not-too-distant future you're going to have to come to this dump and suffer Swat the Kids Night too.'

She didn't answer, maybe because she was horrified at the thought of what I'd said, maybe because she hadn't learnt words yet.

Unfortunately, we found Mum and Dad sooner rather than later. They'd been looking for us too because only I knew which teachers we were booked to see, and after I'd got an earful from Mum we started queuing to see the first of my five. I'll gloss over the chat with Mrs Gamble, Mr Lubelski, Mr Flowerdew the Science teacher and Mr Staples the Away-with-the-Fairies honcho. Mrs G and Mr L were full of praise for me as always, Mr Flowerdew did his best to give me a better-than-hopeless report, and Mr Staples wondered who the hell I was, even though he spends an hour a week looking at the top of my head while it dozes on my desk.

Which brings me to the other teacher I'd had to choose. I'd been hoping to get away with just four, but Dakin examined the lists before signing off on them and told me to add one more. He named three teachers I never had any lessons with, plus Mr Rice and Mr Worzel, which meant it had to be Mr Worzel in spite of his subject. Mr W was quite lively and he liked us to call him Dave, which we assumed was his name rather than his therapist's. Dave W had joined Ranting Lane as a temp when Mr Hurley, our regular History bore, took three months off to lecture on a cruise ship, but when Hurley decided that he liked life at sea more than at Ranting Lane, DW was given total control of his desk and tea mug. There were two people in front of us: Julia Frame, who's in my class, and her mother, who isn't.

'Bit of a scruff for a teacher, isn't he?' Dad whispered while we waited our turn.

'He's my role model,' I said.

'What's his name?'

'Mr Worzel.'

Dad chuckled. 'Worzel? You'd think he'd tidy himself up with a name like that.' *

Just then the Frames moved away, and Dad stepped forward.

'Mr Gummidge,' he said, stretching out a hand.

'Worzel,' said Dave, taking it with a forced smile.

'Sorry, you must get that a lot,' said Dad.

'Not so much these days, no,' said DW.

Then the five of us were sitting on four chairs round his little table like we were about to share an invisible milk shake.

'Dare I ask how Jiggy's doing in History?' Mum asked, getting right to it instead of talking about the weather for five minutes like a normal person.

'Oh, he's quite a star,' Dave answered.

'No need to be sarcastic,' I muttered.

---

*In my parents' distant youth there was a storybook scarecrow called Worzel Gummidge. I know about him because Mum used to read Worzel Gummidge stories to me when I was too young to demand to hear stuff from my childhood rather than hers.

'Sarcastic?' he said. 'I mean it. You're one sharp history student.'

Dad turned to me. 'You can get in trouble for bribing teachers, Jig. I should know, I tried it. Almost got expelled.'

Dave laughed. 'He didn't need to bribe me. True, he seems to be attracted to some facets of history more than others, certain periods, but that's understandable. I'm not entranced by the entire panoply myself.'

Mum looked puzzled. 'But he's never been good at History. Any of it.'

'Well, he's certainly getting into it now,' Dave said. 'He's even picked me up on one or two historical details.'

Mum gripped dad's arm like she might pass out. Dad gripped hers for the same reason. I would have gripped Swoozie's, but she only has little arms. Praise for Art and English had been expected, but History? That was a real first.

'Do me a favour,' I said to the Golden Oldies as we left the hall. 'Don't mention this to anyone.'

'Mention it?' said Mum. 'I'm thinking of fixing a banner to the front of the house.'

I grabbed her wrist, all set to give her a Chinese burn. 'Seriously. Don't mention it. Specially when Pete's about. If one word reaches either of his ears I'm joining the ranks of the homeless – OK?'

When we got home, Mum remembered an envelope that had come for me that morning. It was an A4 envelope with GIT in the corner.

I groaned. 'Oh, not another one.'

'Quite a day for history, eh?' Mum said, eyes glowing. 'Open it, Jig.'

'Later,' I said, snatching the thing and trudging up to my room.

The reason she'd said 'Quite a day for history' was because GIT stood for Genetic Investigations in Time, and Genetic Investigations in Time was a company that could run a person's DNA through its computers and find ancestors who were as like that person as anyone can get in another century. And that's what they'd done with the sample of my DNA that my mother had squeezed out of my trap one night while I was in Slumberville. The first I knew about any of this was when my parents handed me GIT envelope number one on my birthday and I found this old-fashioned type scroll inside which mentioned a 15th-century ancestor.* I couldn't have cared less about someone who lived that long ago, of course, but in a weak moment I looked up some info about that time, and then a bit more, and so on until, in History one day, I told Mr Worzel that he'd got something wrong about 15th-century life. Ruined my class cred in a stroke, specially with Garrett, who said he would never let me hear the last of it. Boys aren't supposed to contribute in lessons like History, you see. It's one of those unwritten rules that no one's ever read.

Pete gave me such a hard time that I vowed not to make the same mistake when the second scroll arrived. That didn't look like being a problem because scroll two mentioned an ancestor in the early 20th century, which interested me even less than the 15th.** But then – wouldn't you know it! – we had to go on that class trip to the Edwardian Life Exhibition, and next thing I know I'm checking out the sort of junk an Edwardian Jiggy might've had lobbed at him. I kept very quiet about it, thought no one had noticed, but Dave

---

*See the first Jiggy's Genes book: *Jiggy's Magic Balls.*
**See the second Jiggy's Genes book: *Jiggy the Vampire Slayer.*

Worzel must have or he wouldn't have told my parents what he did.

Well, it had to stop. My interest in history was in the past, where it belonged. Once I knew when the third Jiggy-type oldster lived I would concentrate on today and today only. I glared at myself in my wall mirror to make sure I understood this. I even raised a stern eyebrow to get the message well and truly across. Then I ripped open the envelope and pulled out the scroll. As with the first two, there wasn't much information.

17th century. Date of birth mid-1630s. Parents almost certainly involved in the English Civil War. Research shows some affiliation with witchcraft.

Witchcraft? I thought. What would someone like me be doing with witchcraft? All that I knew about witches was that they flew about on broomsticks and cackled while stirring bubbly stuff in big black cauldrons. As for the English Civil War, I vaguely remembered Mr Hurley telling us something about it, but because it was Hurley it had been so boring that it had gone in one ear and right out the other one in two and a half seconds flat.

I shoved the scroll back in the envelope. Mum would expect to be shown it before she went to bed, and when she saw it she was sure to go over the top and say something like, 'Wow, 17th century, English Civil War, witchcraft, how fascinating.'

Well, if she was so fascinated, let her think about it. I'd had it with history. History was getting me a bad rep. Anyway, what did I care about someone who was mixed up in old wars and witchy stuff? Less than zero, that's how much.

Even if he was my exact double.

JIGGY AND THE WITCHFINDER

AS TOLD BY THE
17TH-CENTURY JIGGY

I'm an only child, my name's Jidgey O'Dear, and neither of those things is my fault. Jidgey was the name of a saint who did some holy stuff in some place I'd never been. I once asked my parents why they'd called me after a saint. 'Oh, we rather liked it,' they said. 'And it is unusual.' They might have liked it, and it might have been unusual, but it wasn't until I was about ten that my mother discovered that St Jidgey was a sort of nun. Yes, my parents gave me a female nun's name! I ordered them to keep quiet about that if they wanted me to ever speak to them again.

My folks aren't like normal people. Even my nan says that, and she's Mum's mother. I'd been sent to stay with Nan in her village in East Anglia because of the war. The war hadn't got that far, which meant it was pretty quiet there. *Too* quiet actually. The village's name was Great Piddle. That's right,

Great Piddle. And the village down the road was called Little Piddle. The villages were called that because the neighbourhood river was...wait for it...the River Piddle.

Little Piddle was actually bigger than Great Piddle. Nan told me that it was called 'Little' because the river got really narrow there. The narrow bit fed into a pond known as Piddle Pond, which never ran dry, even when there was a drought on, like when I was there. It hadn't rained for weeks and the river was absolutely waterless, but the pond was as full as ever. It's important that you know this because of what I'm going to tell you here.

Now the war. One lot of English people fighting another lot of English people. Nan didn't think much of it. Said it was a bunch of stupid men with long hair (mostly) fighting stupid men with short hair (mostly). My dad was one of the stupid short-haired ones, and so was Mum, though she wasn't a man. She'd lopped her mop before going off with Dad to fight, but she got really narked when people called her a Roundhead. 'What would you prefer, Squarehead?' Dad asked, and she thumped him.

Fierce lady, my mum. You wouldn't want to be on the other side when she came at you waving a sword or firing a musket. Given the chance, my dad would stop for a chat about cloud formations or something, but Mum would have the chatty enemy's head off and stomp it into the mud before he could get any further than 'They say it'll be raining by the end of the aftern—'

Mum and Dad's side had won the war, but they hadn't come for me yet. They said there was a lot of clearing up to do (whatever that meant), so I had to put up with Great Piddle for the time being. It wasn't so bad there. Nan was all right. Her name was Kat Butterby, and she was tall and lean like Mum, and her hair was still dark, also like Mum's, and she had a black cat which I'd heard people call Kat's cat, though his name was Sly.

'Why's he called that?' I asked the first time I saw the mog.

'He's called Sly,' Nan explained, 'because from the day he strayed onto my doorstep he was always sneaking food away when he thought I wasn't looking. He still does, to this day, even though he's well fed.'

Nan also had a fancy man, Frankie Merk, though he wasn't really very fancy. Frankie and Nan got together after he came to her for something to cure a wart in a very Merky place. She gave him one of her ointments and he said that if it worked he'd come back and attend to whatever jobs she needed doing about the house. 'Thought that'd be the last I saw of him,' Nan told me shortly after I went to stay with her, 'but a week later, back he comes, all smiles. "It did the trick!" he says. He was very happy not to have to stand up all the time any more, and he kept his word about doing them jobs. Been here ever since.'

Frankie wasn't bold and tough like Nan, and he was shorter than her, and bald apart from a pair of side bits, but they laughed a lot together. Nan liked a laugh. She had a nice little cottage, with a good garden full of herbs and things. One corner of the garden was given over to itchycoo plants. The itchycoo was well-named because if you crushed its pods and rubbed them on someone's back you could give them a really insane itch. I knew this because when I was younger me and my mates did it all the time. Nan didn't grow itchycoo to make itching powder, though. Quite the opposite. By boiling the pods and adding a handful of secret ingredients, she made a cream that kept itches at bay.

It was just as well Nan knew how to make anti-itch cream because there was an outbreak of extreme itchiness while I was staying with her. No one knew what caused it or where it came from, but some folk blamed it on the Royalists. Said that as they'd lost the war they were spreading it in anti-Royalist regions like ours as a punishment. Nan would have none of it.

'It's just one of them things,' she said. 'Like summer colds, measles, infestations of ladybirds. Next year there'll be an outbreak of headaches, or boils. Will they blame that on the Royalists too?'

'I know I will,' chuckled Frankie Merk.

Whatever it was and whatever caused it, the Big Itch didn't get everyone, the three of us included. But every morning Nan sent Frankie off with a handcart full of itchycoo cream for those that had got it bad. He carried other ointments and medicines too, but the itchycoo cream was the most wanted product just then, so she called him the Itchfinder General. Nan only charged if her customers had money. If they were skint she did a trade, which meant she sometimes had more turnips and carrots and eggs than she and Frankie (and me when I stayed with them) could chomp in a month of Mondays. One customer was so grateful to be free of the Big Itch that he gave her half a pig. I felt sorry for the other half. Can't be easy standing on two legs instead of the usual four, or snorting with half a snout.

Like I said, life was unbelievably quiet in Great Piddle, and as there was a shortage of boys my own age I spent most of my days and hours and minutes bored out of my walnut. But one day of early August, the sun hammering down like it had for weeks, things got a lot less quiet, and stayed that way for most of the next day too. It started when Nan sent me to Little Piddle to get some honey from a lady called Widow Atterbury.

'Give her this tub of ointment in exchange,' she said.

'Has she got the Big Itch?' I asked.

'This isn't itchycoo cream. It's for her veronicas.'

'Veronicas? She has more than one daughter called Veronica?'

'Not daughters, verrucas. Foot warts. She calls them veronicas. You'll have to ask for directions when you get to Little Piddle because Honey Cottage is quite tucked away. But she's expecting you.'

'Expecting me? How do you know?

Nan grinned. 'I'm a witch.'

She didn't mean it, of course. It was just one of those things she said.

On the way out I passed Frankie Merk. He was by the gate loading his handcart. He saw the tub of ointment I was tucking into the bag on my shoulder.

'You bin given a task too, Jidg?' he said.

'Stuff for Widow Atterbury's veronicas.'

He smiled. 'Batty old Tilly.'

'Tilly?'

'Widow Atterbury. My cousin. Don't see a lot of one another these days. It's them bees of hers. Not a great one for bees, me.'

As I went through the gate I almost tripped over Nan's cat. He'd probably seen me coming and thrown himself across the gate to trip me.

'Hi, Sly, what's a'purring?' I said, jumping over him just in time.

He bared his fangs, like he was saying, 'Touch me, son, and you lose a knuckle.' Sly was not a friendly feline. Not with me anyway.

It was about half a mile to Little Piddle on a twisty dirt road, but it seemed longer on a warm day like that. By the time I got there my throat felt like old parchment, so I was pretty keen to find Widow Atterbury's and beg a drink. I might even have taken a sip of river water if there'd been any. The river ran through the centre of the village but it was so dry now that you could've ignored the two little bridges that crossed it and jumped down and strolled across without so much as a squelch. There was no one about to ask the way to Honey Cottage, but as it turned out I didn't need to look for anyone because someone found me – by tossing a bowlful of water out of a window I was passing under.

I glared up through my dripping hair. A girl was looking down.

'Sorry,' she said. 'Didn't see you there.'

'Well, it's good to know you didn't do it

deliberately,' I said, plucking unhappily at my wet clothes.

'Are you lost?' she asked.

'Before, I was lost. Now I'm lost and wet.'

'Where you trying to get to?'

'I'm looking for Widow Atterbury's.'

'Honey Cottage?'

'Yeah.'

'It's not easy to find,' she said. 'I'll show you if you like.'

'Just point the way, will you?' I was pretty annoyed actually.

'It's no trouble, I got nothing better to do.'

She left the window before I could argue further and was down in no time, leading me across one of the little bridges over the waterless river. On the opposite bank, she told me her name.

'Dolly Byrd. What's yours?'

'Jidgey O'Dear.'

'Oh dear.'

I sighed. Everyone said that.

At the far end of the village Dolly Byrd showed me to a wall of overgrown cow parsley.

'Go through,' she said.

'What?'

'Go through.'

'Why would I do that?'

'Because it's the way to Widow Atterbury's.'

'It could also be just one step from the edge of a cliff.'

'Bold, aren't you?' she said, sweeping the cow parsley aside and holding it back like a curtain.

I looked through, to a narrow footpath bordered on both sides by weeds and grass at least as high as the cow parsley.

'How far?' I asked, starting along the path.

'All the way,' Dolly said, following.

We walked in silence for a time. When the silence got really deafening I asked what happened to Mr Atterbury.

'Mr Atterbury?'

'Widow Atterbury's husband.'

'There never was a Mr Atterbury.'

'There must've been. Why else would she be called Widow Atterbury?'

'Widow Atterbury's no more a widow than Honey Cottage is a cottage,' Dolly said. 'She's never been married. Decided when she was about nine that she liked the idea of being a widow, and the name stuck. Some rain'd be nice.'

The sudden change of subject made me miss a step.

'Rain?'

'Specially if it fell on you.'

'Why on me especially?'

'It'd wash off the water I threw over you.'

'Why would it need to? Water's water.'

'Not necessarily,' she said.

'How do you mean?'

'The stuff drying on you isn't exactly...'

'Exactly what?'

'Pure.'

'I don't get you.'

'It was from the chamber pot under my bed.'

'The what?'

'The chamber pot under my bed.'

I stopped. So did she.

'The water you threw over me was from the chamber pot under your bed?'

'Yes.'

'And the chamber pot was full of...'

'Well, not *full*. But full enough. Sorry.'

I looked down at myself.

'Eeeerrrgh!'

My feet started to dance and my arms got all flappy like I'd got a dose of the Big Itch.

I was covered in pee!

Head to toe.

And it wasn't even my own!

When I managed to stop jigging about I looked at the sky. It was blue. Very blue. Not a cloud in it. Not a *hint* of cloud.

'I don't think it's going to rain ever again,' I said.

'Not today anyway,' Dolly said. 'But as it happens, you're in luck.'

I stared at her. 'Luck? I'm covered in pee. Your pee. How is that lucky? And why were you chucking potty water into the street anyway?'

'It has to go somewhere,' she said.

'It did go somewhere. Over me.'

'Well how was I to know you were walking under my window? I'm not psychic.'

'But you have eyes. You could have leaned out and used them – *before* you threw the pee rather than afterwards.'

'There's not usually any need to look. Little Piddlers don't walk under windows.'

'Oh, I wonder why?' I said.

'And we don't get many visitors.'

'If this is how you greet them I'm not surprised. I need to wash this off. I really, really, *really* need to wash this off.'

'Yes. And like I said, you're in luck with that.' Dolly parted the tall grass on one side of the path, and said: 'Piddle Pond.'

Piddle Pond was big, and full of water of the non-pee variety. I barged through the grass and bent over the water to splash my head and body and everything I was wearing.

'WHAT DO YOU THINK YOU'RE DOING?!'

I jumped. Looked along the bank. A scrawny woman with a long nose and shoulders as sharp as her question knelt there, glaring at me.

'He needed a wash, Miss Nutter,' Dolly Byrd told the woman.

'I don't care what he needed!' the woman snapped. 'He's broken my concentration. Get him out of here. At once!'

'Come on,' Dolly said to me.

'In a minute,' I said, splashing and splashing, sploshing and sploshing.

'I said GO!' the woman shouted in her thin tight voice. 'NOW!'

Dolly grabbed my wet arm and lugged me back onto the path. I heard the woman say something nasty as the grass closed behind us.

'What's her problem?' I asked as we continued on our way.

'She's a Nutter,' said Dolly.

'She's that all right.'

'No, it's her name. She's Fanny Nutter. Sister of Isobel.'

'Never heard of her. Either of them.'

'You're new around here then, are you?'

'I'm staying with my nan in Great Piddle.'

'Oh. Well, Isobel Nutter was burned as a witch about a year ago, on the village green.'

'Burned? I thought witches were hanged.'

'It was a cold day.'

'Was she really a witch?'

'Isobel was always threatening to hurt people she didn't care for, which was almost everyone, so whenever Little Piddlers got anything wrong with their bottoms, or a runny nose or something, they said it was Issy Nutter's doing. It would have been, too, if she could have managed it. She wasn't a nice woman.'

'Her sister doesn't seem much of a charmer either.'

'No. Fanny Nutter wouldn't be charming even if she hadn't sworn to get the people who cooked her sis.'

'Didn't she try to stop them doing that?'

'She was away at the time. Stirring things up in the war, they say.'

'Which side?'

'Both, probably. Like Isobel, Fanny isn't much of a people person.'

'Was Isobel the only Little Piddle witch?'

'She was one of four accused of witchcraft. The other three were chums of hers. They would meet two or three times a week and sit around cackling loudly to annoy the neighbours. They were just a sewing circle with a bad attitude really, but then Richard Brayne the cobbler put it about that their stitches were spells and bad-luck charms, and they were rounded up and tried as witches by Grimstone Hargreaves.'

'Who's he?'

'One of those witchfinders that ride around looking for people to pick on. He had them dunked in Piddle Pond. You know how the dunking of suspected witches works?'

'Yes. Women accused of witchcraft—'

'Not just women. Men can be witches too.'

'—are thrown into deep water and if they drown they're guilty.'

'No, no. If they *don't* drown they're guilty. If they drown they're innocent. Bit late to apologise then, of course.'

'And the other three ladies of the sewing circle...?'

'Drowned and were thus deemed innocent. Issy was the only one who wouldn't drown. Hargreaves had her thrown in four times – egged on by some of the villagers – and each time she came up spluttering and cursing. The curses must have worked, too, at least as far as Hargreaves was concerned because as he was leaving after burning her he was struck by lightning.'

'Killed?'

'Grilled.'

'So what's Isobel's sister doing at Piddle Pond?'

'Trying to call up the demon Issy summoned as she surfaced for the fourth time.'

'Demon!'

'That's what she claimed to be doing. Theory has it that the demon arrived too late and sank to the bottom because Issy was gone and there was no one to command him. Fanny's been trying to coax him out ever since to deal with Richard Brayne and the others who accused her sister. No sign of him so far.'

'I'm surprised they haven't tried to burn her as a witch,' I said.

'They wouldn't dare. On her good days, Fanny's more terrifying than Issy on her worst. No one has the guts to suggest dropping her in the pond to see if she floats, least of all Dick Brayne. Oh – bees!'

'Eh?'

'There.'

A mass of bees had risen over a wall of grass that blocked the way ahead. Having risen, they hovered like they were getting set to fly at us.

'Widow Atterbury's watchbees,' Dolly said. 'They'll only attack if they think we're up to no good.'

'How do we prove we're not?'

'We just walk ahead, all casual like, and smiling.'

She pushed her way gently through the grass and I followed her into a little garden with half a dozen beehives and a door in the side of a rock face.

'She lives in a hill?' I asked Dolly.

'A cave. Now you know why you'd never've found Honey Cottage on your own.'

She knocked on the door, which was opened almost at once by a tiny woman with the wrinkliest face I ever saw. Some of the wrinkles were smiles. She looked like a very smiley person.

'Dolly Byrd! Good to see you. Who's your friend?'

'Diddy O'My,' Dolly said. 'He was looking for you.'

'Jidgey O'Dear,' I corrected.

Widow Atterbury looked me up and down. 'You're wet,' she said.

'Warm day,' I said.

'What can I do for you, sonny?'

I took the tub of ointment out of my bag. 'My nan asked me to bring you this in exchange for some honey.'

'Your nan?'

'Kat Butterby. I'm staying with her.'

'Oh, I see, for my veronicas. Come in, come in!'

It was like a normal cottage inside, except for a bit of a window shortage. There was even a fireplace, with a small fire in the grate. Dry turf. Sweet, earthy smell. Widow Atterbury went to a shelf lined with jars of honey and handed me one. I put it in my bag.

'Would you like a nice cool drink?' she asked.

'We would,' said Dolly.

The old dear took a brown earthenware jug and poured us a beaker each of something home-made. Cow parsley cordial, she called it. It wasn't bad, and it went down a treat after all that walking. As Dolly and I left her at her front door a few minutes later, bees buzzed towards us. I ducked.

'They're just curious about you,' Widow A said. 'Walk straight ahead and they won't touch you.'

The bees flew with us to the high grass gate but no further. Dolly and I headed back along the footpath. In a minute we heard someone reciting something on the pond side of the grass. We peered through. Fanny Nutter stood on the bank, eyes shut, arms outstretched, chanting.

'O mighty demon in the pond,
Summoned from the great beyond,
Let me see your frabjous face,
In this poor benighted place.
Rise up now from e'er ye dwell,
Do my bidding, hear my spell,
Lend your awesome powers to me—'

'Then shove off home and leave us be!'

The last line wasn't Miss Nutter's, it was mine. I couldn't resist it. Dolly squawked and Miss N whirled. 'WHO WAS THAT?!' she screamed as the grasses sprang back and covered our faces. Well, my face. Dolly was already away. I was about to start after her when a skinny arm came through the grass and gripped me by the throat. The Nutter features plunged through a second later.

'You again!' she cried.

'Eeeeerk,' I replied, struggling for breath.

'It's taken me months to get the demon-calling spell right!' she shrieked. 'I was close to a breakthrough! That close' – she gave my throat an extra squeeze – 'and you RUINED it!'

She flung my throat away, sending me flying. I would have scrambled to my feet and done a swift runner, but before I could get up she'd bounded through the grass and was standing over me, glaring down with the darkest eyes I ever saw. Fanny Nutter was one terrifying lady.

'Couldn't you just start again?' I asked, propping myself up on one elbow and massaging my squeezed throat.

'It's not just the *words*!' she screeched. 'A very particular mood must be conjured to summon demons, and your delinquent interference has destroyed mine utterly! It could take days to reach such a state again!'

'Look, I'm sorry,' I said. 'But if it's all the same to you, I'll be going now.'

I got to my feet and turned away.

'Wait!'

I glanced back. 'What?'

'Kneel and beg my forgiveness.'

She pointed a long bony finger at the ground so I'd know exactly what she meant.

'I already apologised,' I said.

'Not good enough. Kneel and beg.'

'Beg? I don't think so. My mum doesn't believe in begging.'

I started away. But something hard and bony gripped my shoulder. A Nutter hand. Which whirled me round to face her.

'You refuse to kneel?' she said, shoving her skinny face into mine. Her breath smelt like last week's boiled cabbage.

'I do,' I said, hoping I sounded bolder than I felt.

I would have turned away again, but when I tried to I found that I couldn't move. Her eyes were like magnets, holding me there. But then she blinked, and so did I, and she spun me around and gave me a small shove. I started walking. But then...

I fell to my knees.

A screechy laugh behind me. 'Won't kneel for me, eh?' Miss Nutter cackled.

I got up. Started forward. My knees folded. Down I went. Again I got to my feet, and this time I used them to run with. They ran about three yards before my knees hit the ground once more. Miss Nutter's cackle rose to a high pitch of delight behind me.

I got up again. I ran again. I fell again. I got up, ran, fell, got up, ran, fell, again and again and again, and every knee-drop brought another howl of Nutter laughter. Laughter that followed me all the way along the path.

'She *is* a witch!' I said, falling to my knees at the end.

Dolly was there, waiting. She helped me up. 'What happened?'

'She put a spell on me!'

Five yards further on I once again kneed it. Dolly hauled me to my feet and supported me till I fell once more. She helped me up, supported me till I fell, and so on until I told her not to bother because supporting me didn't stop me falling. I could no longer hear Miss Nutter's laughter by then and I'm glad to say that the further I got from her the longer I could go between knee-drops. By the time we reached Dolly's house I was doing about ten yards between falls.

'Want me to walk you home?' she asked.

'No point,' I said, falling to my knees.

'All right.' She headed for her front door. 'Have a nice day!'

Nice day. Ha! If only. I had no idea that my day was only just *beginning* to unravel. Worse was yet to come.

A whole lot worse.

I was only doing the knee-ground routine every twenty yards or so by the time I made it to Nan's, but I can't say this made me happy. Twice more I'd tried running between falls, hoping to race through the next one, and twice my legs had given way, so I'd given up running as a bad job. Nan was at the gate, jawing with this weedy ginger-bearded geezer beside a big horse-drawn cart piled high with old rubbish. I'd seen the Antiques Roadcart before, and the owner, whose name was Eebay Tatt. Mr Tatt drove around buying stuff on the cheap or pulling it out of ditches and selling it on to anyone stupid enough to buy it. I was surprised to see my nan looking at his junk.

'Too far for your little legs?' Nan asked as I fell to my knees.

'Long story,' I said.

'Get my honey, honey?'

I tugged out the jar, which by some miracle hadn't smashed with all my falls. I put it on the wall by the gate.

'What do you think of this?' Nan asked, elbowing a chair Mr Tatt had taken down from his cart. It was an ordinary kitchen type chair – high wooden back, rush seat – but I was suspicious of anything from the Roadcart.

'You want to check it won't collapse under you, like my legs,' I said.

'Cor-larps?' said Eebay Tatt like he was offended. 'Nuthina mine'll cor-larps, lad.' Then he gave me a twisted black-toothed smirk that as good as said 'with any luck'. He wore a floppy brown hat whose brim looked like bites had been taken out of it, and had the dirtiest shirt collar I ever saw. When he talked he rubbed one hand over the other all the time like they couldn't wait to count the money.

'Give it a try, Jidgey,' Nan said.

'Better if I fall through it than you, eh?' I said.

She beamed. 'You're younger.'

'The lad don't need ta sit arn it,' said Mr Tatt. He looked a bit worried all of a sudden.

'I think he should,' said Nan. 'Just in case.' She

gave me a wink. 'You test the chair while I go see if Mr T has anything else worth having today.'

While they went round the back of the cart I gave the chair a shake. It seemed sound enough. I got down and checked the struts between the legs. They were well fixed. Which left just one more thing to try. I parked myself on the rush seat. The chair didn't even wobble. I was about to stand up when I saw Mr Tatt peering at me from behind the cart, so I gave a really mighty wriggle in the chair, just for him. It didn't collapse, but it did something else.

It threw me.

Suddenly I was on the ground again, but not on my knees this time, and not in front of the chair. Nowhere near it, in fact. The chair was nowhere to be seen. Nor was the Antiques Roadcart, or Mr Tatt, or my nan, or her cottage. I was in the middle of a field surrounded by cows. Sitting in something soft and squishy that didn't smell too sweet.

A fresh cowpat.

I pulled myself – *sssshhhlukkk!* – out of the pat and stared at the bott-shaped impression I'd made in it. I carried on staring as it oozed back into its normal shape, until no one would know it had been near any back end except a cow's.

I looked about me. I knew this field. It belonged to the farm behind the cottage. I started back, as baffled as a blind bat in a black box. How had I got from Mr Tatt's chair to a steaming cowpat in that field? Had Miss Nutter put a second spell on me? A spell that would fling me into the nearest cowpat every time I sat down? This is what I was thinking when I fell to my knees – not to pray, but because I once again couldn't help it. I fell to them twice more before I reached the road and met Mr Tatt driving his horse and cart away from Nan's.

'Bin some'ere, boy?' he asked.

There was something about the glint in his bright little eyes that made me suspicious.

'That chair of yours...' I said.

A dry chuckle bubbled up from his scrawny throat. 'Gled ta see the beck o' thet chair, I em. Folks keep bringin' it beck arter they brought it, dun ax me why.'

He was still chuckling as he drove away. That clinched it. It was the chair that had patted my backside and Mr Tatt knew it because I wasn't the first it had done something like that to.

I shook my head. First Miss Nutter and her knee-fall spell. Now a tossing chair. Whatever next?

Whatever next was something I would've been glad never to hear about unless it happened to someone else. Unfortunately, it was going to happen to me. Me and one other.

'Where'd you go?' Nan asked when I got back. 'One minute you was there, the next you wasn't.'

'That chair,' I said, looking at it, standing all innocent by the gate. 'It threw me into the field.'

Nan thought this was very funny. For a minute. Then she sniffed.

'Jidgey, what's that smell?!'

'The cowpat I landed in.'

'You fell in a cowpat?'

'The chair threw me into one.'

'Oh, what nonsense you talk,' she said. 'Take it inside for me. Then we'll see about warming some water to soak them pants.'

'No, listen,' I said. 'Trust me, you don't want this chair indoors.'

'It won't be stopping,' she said. 'I got it for Frankie's cart. Some of my patients are getting on a bit and I thought they'd be glad of a sit-down while he's talking to 'em on his rounds. Take it in, there's a good boy.'

'They might not be glad they sat in *this* chair,' I muttered, starting up the path with it. I was about halfway to the step when I fell to my knees and the chair flew sideways, into a patch of patchouli.

'Jidgey, be careful, you'll break it.'

'What about me?'

'I didn't pay for you,' she said.

I yanked the chair out of the patchouli. 'Nan,' I said. 'That's not me being clumsy. A spell's been put on me that makes me fall down. I met a stringy old bird called Fanny Nutter and I said something she didn't like and now I fall to my knees every few yards.'

Nan's eyes clouded over. 'Fanny Nutter?'

'Yes. It's not as bad as it was, but I only started falling down after I had a run-in with her.'

'And the cowpat?'

'That was the chair.'

'You and that chair,' she said. 'I'll not hear any more about that. But Fanny Nutter, oh now, she's a different matter.'

'You know her then?'

'I've known Fanny since we was gals. Her and her awful sister.'

'The one that got toasted?'

'Yes. I wouldn't wish that on anyone, but Issy Nutter's no loss, and nor would Fanny be neither. So. Made you fall down, did she?'

'You believe me?'

She nodded. 'It's not a spell, though. Fanny can't do spells. Thinks she can, tries all the time, but the most she can manage is planting suggestions in feeble minds. Did you look into her eyes?'

'I couldn't not, she was standing over me.'

'Well that's how she did it. And I can do the same thing. Look at me, boy.'

I was already looking at her, but now her eyes locked onto mine and I couldn't even blink until she did. Then she said, 'You'll not fall down again.'

She was right. I didn't fall down again. I didn't say any more about Eebay Tatt's chair either. Wasn't worth the bother. When Frankie Merk came in he tried the chair to see how it felt, and it didn't throw him. Which got me thinking. Maybe it wasn't the chair that had turfed me into the field.

But if it wasn't the chair, what else could have done it? Was it a side effect of the falling-down thing Miss Nutter had eyeballed into my mind? If that was it, and Nan had got rid of it, the chair would be as safe for me now as it was for Frankie. I needed to test that. Without an audience.

That night, some time after Nan and Frankie went to bed, I crept downstairs. I sat down in the chair kind of nervously, half expecting to be back in the cowpat any second. But nothing happened. I sat there, all still and tense, expecting the worst – until I remembered that last time, Mr Tatt had been watching me like he knew something was going to happen, and because his eyes were on me I'd given a massive wriggle to show him I was giving his chair a good going-over. It was during the massive wriggle that it happened.

So I gritted my teeth and gave a big wriggle once again.

And guess what.

I lurched.

The room disappeared.

The O'Dear rear crashed to the ground in the same field as before.

The good news was that this time there was no under-bum squelch. I was over by the bramble hedge that ran round the field.

So it *was* the chair!

CHAPTER FOUR

I overslept next morning. No surprise after being up in the night. Nan didn't wake me. She's good like that. My mother screams at me to get up around dawn every day, but when I'm at Nan's she lets me lie in as long as I want most of the time.

When I went down I seemed to be the only one in apart from Sly. He was on the windowsill, like an ornament. The front door was open. I looked out and saw a bunch of Great Piddlers on the village green. Nan and Frankie were among them, on the edge of the crowd. Frankie had his handcart. Sitting up on it was Eebay Tatt's chair. I grabbed a hunk of bread and mooched over to see what was going on. Sly jumped off the sill and mooched with me. He didn't usually go anywhere with me, so I felt quite flattered.

The villagers were gathered round a stranger, a young man somewhere in the second half of his twenties. He was quite slight, with a short beard trimmed to a point, and he wore a wide-brimmed hat, a linen-collared shirt and a black cape. He fingered a silver-handled walking stick while he talked. The stick was crooked and gnarled and didn't match anything else about him. From the look of him and the first words I heard as I drew near, I took him for a wandering preacher who'd been on the road too long for his health. I mention his health because every so often he coughed nastily, not always into his hand, which made his audience lean back so as not to catch his germs.

'These are dark and dreadful days,' the man was saying. 'While bloody civil war raged about us, the Devil's minions brought chaos, pestilence and drought, and the evil ones are among us still.'

'What are you getting at?' an irked voice said. 'Come now, plain English, we haven't got all day to stand here listening to gibberish.'

That was my nan. Nan hates people putting on airs and graces and talking fancy like this character was doing. He went up on tiptoe to pick her out over nearer heads.

'What I'm saying, madam, is that there's

witchcraft in this region, and I'm here to stamp it out.'

When he said 'witchcraft' his head jerked sideways, very sharply like he'd been slapped, but he hardly paused, just carried on like head-jerking was one of those things that went with the job.

Nan tutted. 'Witchcraft! Get ye gone, man. Bother others with your superstitious twaddle!'

'Superstitious twaddle?' The man seemed offended. 'I tell you, blasphemers insinuate themselves into society and conjure all manner of wickedness to take us from the righteous road.'

'Righteous Road's that way,' Nan said, pointing out of the village. 'Attach your holier-than-us heels to it, and sharpish. We want no talk like yours in the Piddles.'

The visitor clearly liked this even less. He pushed his way forward and the crowd parted to let him through. Reaching Nan, he looked like he was about to give her a mouthful when he noticed the chair on Frankie's cart.

'What's this?' he demanded, rapping it with his stick.

'Well, it's for sittin' on,' Frankie answered. A few

people tittered, but the stranger wasn't one of them. He picked up one of Nan's tubs of ointment and turned it round in his hand.

'And this?'

'Itchycoo cream,' said Frankie.

'And it does what, precisely?'

'It cures itches.'

'He's the Itchfinder General!' someone said, probably to lighten things up. Again, one or two laughed. The stranger leaned towards Frankie.

'Do you mock me, fellow?'

Frankie stepped back. 'Mock you?'

'I take it you know who I am?'

Frankie shook his head. 'Not a clue, mate.'

'I am Matthew Hopkins.'

'Never heard of you,' Frankie said.

'I have,' said Nan. She twisted her mouth like it had something nasty in it. 'So. Hopkins the witchfinder is among us.'

Master Hopkins narrowed his eyes at her. 'Witchfinder *General*!' he snarled, jerking his head sideways.

'Self-*appointed* Witchfinder General!' Nan snarled back.

'I am appointed by Parliament,' said the gentleman.

'That's not what I heard.'

'Then you heard wrongly, madam.'

'Prove it.'

'Prove what?'

'That Parliament appointed you.'

'I need prove nothing to you,' he said. 'But you should perhaps prove something to me.'

'Oh yes? Like what?'

'That you are who you pretend to be.'

'I pretend nothing,' said Nan. 'I am what you see.'

'Yes,' Master Hopkins sneered. 'And what I see...'

A bad coughing fit cut him short. Everyone leaned back politely until he'd got over the worst of it. He was down to the last splutter when he put the tub back in Frankie's cart. 'Is it you, perchance, who makes these potions?' he asked Nan.

'I wouldn't call 'em potions,' she said, 'but yes, they're mine, what of it?'

'I'll tell you what of it, woman. I—'

Again he didn't finish, but not because of his cough this time. Nan's cat, Sly, had jumped up on the cart and hissed at him.

'You have a familiar!' Master Hopkins cried, rearing back.

'Familiar?' said Nan. 'That's just my cat.'

'It might be a cat now. But familiars change shape at will, and when their masters and mistresses go out at night on their wicked errands, they become bats, or imps, or spirits bent on unholy deeds.'

A shocked buzz whipped round the crowd, and a few of the villagers glanced at Nan in ways that seemed to say that Master Hopkins had put into words what they'd thought themselves more than once.

'You're an idiot, Hopkins,' said Nan. 'I suspected as much from what I've heard of you, and now I know it for sure. Get the hell out of our village.'

But Master Hopkins just smiled. A slow, thin, knowing smile. 'Hell,' he said. 'Your master's domain, perhaps?'

Nan reached out and knocked his hat off. Master Hopkins covered his head like he thought she was going to set about him, but all she did was put her hands on her hips and laugh at him.

'On your way, little man! Scoot!'

But instead of scooting, Master Hopkins stooped for his hat, jammed it back on and, glaring at Nan, banged his silver-handled stick on the ground between them. The stick immediately began to shake quite heartily, and when it did this the witchfinder let out a howl that contained a single word.

'Witch!'

His head jerked sideways so hard when he said this that I thought it might spin off his neck.

'That twitch of yours,' Nan said. 'Guilty conscience, that'll be. Every time you say "witch" a little voice in your poor excuse for a brain says "You're doing wrong, Matthew Hopkins, doing wrong".'

'Your blasphemy has no end, woman,' Master Hopkins growled, and turned to the crowd. 'I have a question of you good folk, and I want you to answer truthfully. Has any one of you suffered a change in health or circumstance thanks to this person's intervention?'

'Oh, you fool,' Nan muttered, but then she fell silent, curious to hear what might be said by her fellow villagers.

Goodwife Thorne of Dandelion Cottage was the

first to speak. 'Well, she cured my lumbago,' she said. 'And very grateful I was to her.'

Then Mr Binks the roadmender spoke up. 'Helped me with my gout, she did,' he said, winking at Nan.

'And that itchycoo cream of hers is a wonder,' said a large woman whose name I didn't know.

This was all out before others could hush the speakers.

'Thanks for the testimonials,' Nan said, 'but you've told this specimen just what he wants to hear. Next thing we know he'll accuse me of witchcraft.'

'Witchcraft!' spat a man at the back. 'Ain't no such thing.'

He'd barely got this out when there was a sharp thud followed by a soft moan, and when I craned round the crowd I saw a big beefy stranger standing over a much smaller man who lay at his feet with his eyes shut.

'He should be driven out before he turns us against one another,' Nan said of Master Hopkins. 'But I'll leave that to you. I'll not spend another minute in his presence. Frankie Merk, off on your rounds now!'

Frankie must have been glad to go because while Nan stormed back to her cottage he aimed his cart at the road to Little Piddle and ran off with it like something was after him, the chair from the Antiques Roadcart bobbing about on top. I'd meant to warn him to tell his customers not to move too much in the chair, but it was too late now.

I had worked my way round the crowd during the proceedings I've just described, and on the other side I saw something that Nan can't have or she would have said something. Master Hopkins's horse and cart was parked under the old oak near Vinnie Price's forge, and in the cart sat three women who looked quite a bit less than cheerful. Also in the cart was an empty chair. So that was why Master H had thought Frankie (the Itchfinder General) was mocking him! A young man in a floppy felt hat sat cross-legged on the ground near the horse, tugging at the grass at the edge of the green. I strolled over.

'What's happening?' I asked.

He glanced up. 'Who wants to know?'

It wasn't till he spoke that I realised he wasn't

a lad, but a girl. I guessed she was about nineteen, but I'm no expert on girly ages. She was very pale in spite of weeks of sunshine, and her clothes were all rumpled, like she'd been sleeping in them night after night for ages.

'Just asking,' I said. 'You with Master Hopkins?'

'Yeh.'

'Who are these ladies?'

'Witches.'

'Witches? *Actual* witches?'

'*Suspected* witches. They ent bin tried yet.'

Looking closer, I saw that the women were chained to big iron rings fixed to the insides of the cart. No wonder they looked cheesed off.

'So the two of you travel round looking for witches, do you?' I said.

'The three of us,' the girl answered. 'We was four, but Janey Blaney got fed up of the life and went home last week.'

'Three of you? Where's the third?'

She chinned the crowd on the green. I would have asked who she meant, but she got in first. 'He keeps his head down till he's needed, same as me.'

'What's your job then?' I asked.

'I'm doin' it.'

'What, sitting here?'

'Mindin' the accused. Now is there anythin' else, or…?'

I trooped back to the green.

Master Hopkins was still trying to turn the villagers against my nan, even though she'd gone home.

'Evil cannot be permitted to flourish,' he was saying. 'Perpetrators must be brought to book, all of them, wherever they be found. So as Parliament's representative, I put it to you: could that woman, that maker of potions, be a practitioner of the dark arts?'

'What's a practishner?' said Goody Wilkes.

'A witch,' someone told her.

'Well, she's always *saying* she's one,' Goody said.

'It's Kat's little joke,' said another woman, frowning at her.

'If she claims to be a witch,' Master Hopkins said with a jerk, 'and if that cat is her familiar, it's my sacred and patriotic duty to add her to the number of accused there.'

He aimed a thumb at the cart under the oak tree.

'They're witches?' said Maurice Dancer the blacksmith.

'Not yet condemned, but certainly accused,' he was told. 'When we find water of some depth we'll see if they swim.'

'There's no water of any depth round here,' Mr Dancer said. 'Not now. River's all dried up.'

'Piddle Pond's still full,' said Goody Wilkes brightly.

Someone told her to be quiet, but it was too late. Master Hopkins had heard.

'Piddle Pond?' he said with interest. 'Where's that?'

'Just outside Little Piddle,' Goody said. 'Up where Frankie Merk was headed. No distance.'

Two women took Goody aside and whispered urgently to her. She looked shocked, like she hadn't realised she'd spoken out of turn. While Goody was being told what she'd done, Master Hopkins had another of his coughing fits, for once covering his mouth with his cape till it was over.

'You oughta be home in bed with that chest,' said a woman, who I think was called Granny Wilde.

'I was well enough before I set out to expose

witches,' Master Hopkins said, jerking his head. 'They stole my health and may yet be the death of me. Once I'm gone, you can be sure they'll wither your crops and destroy your animals and take all that you have. We must wipe them out with all haste, before they ruin this fine land of ours.'

'This fine land's already ruined, thanks to the war,' said Mr Dancer.

'My business is not politics,' Master Hopkins said, 'but to discover witches.' Again, his head jerked sharply to one side. 'That and nothing more.' He turned back to the others. 'Now I call upon you to fetch that woman back and put her in my cart, and when she's secure I'll take her and the others to the pond and give all four fair trial by water.'

'I'll fetch her,' said someone – the big beefy man I'd noticed before.

'There's a good fellow,' said Matthew Hopkins.

As the man marched to Nan's cottage I heard people asking one another who he was. No one knew him. I sneaked over to Price's forge wishing Mum was there. Mum wouldn't have let Nan be taken out of her home by a strange man, and I bet she would have picked Master Hopkins up by his fancy collar too, and booted his behind all the way out of the village. Afraid of no one, my mum.

Unlike me.

My nan needed someone right now, and all I could do was watch from a safe distance while a stranger ducked into her cottage without an invitation. I wanted to run in after him, grab some crushed itchycoo pods that hadn't been boiled and treated yet, and throw the powder at him so he would itch insanely all over and scratch and scratch and scratch and forget all about bringing Nan back for the witchfinder.

And did I do that?

No. I didn't. I stayed in the doorway of the forge, just watching as the man came out with Nan tucked under his arm like a bundle of washing. Not a quiet or still bundle. She shouted and wriggled and kicked all the way to the witch cart. But it did no good. The man was too big, too strong. He put her in the cart and the girl assistant chained her to one of the iron rings so she couldn't escape. The chain didn't quieten her, though, so Master Hopkins went over and gagged her with a strip of rag. While this was going on, no one, not me or any Great Piddler, made a move to stop it, and then Hopkins addressed his audience once again.

'We've secured one possible Great Piddle witch' – his head jerked – 'but I charge you good people to think, and think well. Is she the only one who might practise the dark arts around here? Search your memories and hearts. Do any others come to mind?'

'Well, I do wonder about—' began Goody Wilkes before Mr Dancer clapped a hand over her mouth and marched her to her cottage.

No one else said anything about possible witches. Everyone looked either shocked or ashamed. A neighbour, someone they'd known all their lives, had been accused of witchcraft and chained up and they'd done nothing to prevent it. They shuffled back to their homes and closed their doors like they wanted to shut out the memory, and in minutes there was only one person left – me, lurking in the shadowy doorway of the forge. The man who'd taken an unplanned nap on the ground had come to and gone indoors, and the stranger who'd knocked him down and captured Nan was already on the road to Little Piddle. So was Master Hopkins and his assistant, with the cartload of women accused of being witches. They were taking my nan to Piddle Pond, where she would either drown or be hanged.

And there was nothing I could do about it.

CHAPTER FIVE

Or was there? There must be somewhere I could get help. But where? Not Great Piddle, obviously. The villagers had shut their doors rather than step in to help her. The only other local person I could think of was Frankie Merk, but devoted as he was to Nan I couldn't see him standing up to Master Hopkins. There was no one else, though. I had to go after Frankie and try and persuade him to do something. But Frankie wasn't the only one on the road to Little Piddle, and as I didn't want to go past the others I took a long cut across the fields, running fast to get ahead of them. This was a pretty desperate thing to do, because running's bad for you. Makes you short of breath, running, and a person needs all the breath he can get. But it had to be done. I had to catch up with Frankie.

I was still running when something small and

black zoomed past me. I only just managed not to leap into a ditch in shock.

'Sly?' I gasped.

He skidded to a halt and flipped round to stare at me. I stared back – nervously. Sly had never attacked me, but there was something in his eyes that made me think he might if I didn't watch my step. Was now that time? Was I about to become a cat snack? When he started towards me I would have gulped if I hadn't already been gulping for three with the breath shortage.

But he didn't attack me. He parked his tail at my jittery feet and stared up at me, all big-eyed and...worried-looking. I'd never seen him look that way before. Summoning all my courage, I bent down, hand outstretched, thinking, 'Well, so-long fingers.' But he didn't snap them off. He put his head against my hand and rubbed it like it was a friend he was glad to have.

'You are *Sly*, aren't you?' I said, puzzled.

'Meooow,' he replied, looking up at me.

'So...what's up?'

'Meooooaaaar.'

'Oh,' I said. 'Right,' I said. 'Yes.'

I'd got it. He'd seen Nan bundled off and chained into the cart and wheeled away with the rest of them. She was the only person he had any time for, probably because she fed him, and he was wondering where the next meal was coming from. He'd run after me because he thought I was going to get her back and make everything right. Some hopes! What could I do against someone as scary as Matthew Hopkins? The best I could hope to do was tell Frankie what had happened and see if he could think of a way to save Nan. He was an adult, after all. Saving people was adult work.

'Gotta run,' I said to Sly.

'Reeeooowl,' he agreed, and off we set again, side by side this time.

Because we were cutting across the fields I knew we were ahead of Master Hopkins as we ran down the slope that concealed the stretch of road he was on. I saw Frankie up ahead. He'd got more of a move on than I expected and was almost in Little Piddle already. I could have called out, but my breath was down to zero again, and besides, a shout might be heard by Master H around the bend behind me.

But there was another reason I didn't want to shout. Between Little Piddle and me and Sly was a crossroads, and riding towards it from another direction were two Royalist troopers. Cavaliers. I'd never seen Cavaliers up close. They were quite a sight. Long hair in ringlets, bright clothes with fancy cuffs and lace collars, plumed hats. The feather in one hat was purple, the one in the other was green. They also wore very big boots.

'You! Lad! Which way to Little Piddle?'

When I didn't answer (still out of breath) the one with the purple feather tugged his horse's reins and clip-clopped over. The horse was huge, which made its rider seem like a towering giant. The uniform and the sword at his belt didn't help put me at my ease. His uniform was a bit worn close up, with a strip of material hanging off one elbow, and his fancy collar and cuffs were torn and dirty. He looked like he'd been in the wars – they both did. Which they had, of course.

'What is it, son? That cat got your tongue?'

Sly can't have liked this because he arched his back and hissed up at the trooper. These men belonged to the king's defeated army, but defeated or not I knew Mum wouldn't like me talking to them. She had no time for Royalists. Or the king. She said the king was a weedy little article with a stupid giggle (she'd heard him speak once) who had no interest in the struggles of ordinary folk like us. She didn't care a whole lot for the leaders on our side either – too pompous and full of God-talk for her – but there were only two sides, and she definitely wasn't going to fall in with those over-privileged aristocracy-lovers, she said. But the trooper leaning over me had a big horse and that sword. I had to answer him.

'It's just up there,' I said. 'Beyond that little cart.'

'Is that where you're going?'

'Yeah.'

'Hop on, I'll give you a lift.'

'No, it's all right, I—'

But he reached down for me and before I knew it I was sitting behind his saddle, on his horse's enormous backside.

'Hold onto my coat,' the trooper said. 'If you don't, you'll fall off.'

His coat might have been in need of a wash and some repair work, but the material wasn't rough like my clothes and the clothes of everyone I knew. Must have been nice being on their side, I thought, and immediately felt guilty for thinking such a thing. Mum would whack me for that.

'We're looking for the lacemaker,' the trooper said over his shoulder as we started off.

'I don't know any lacemaker,' I said.

'We're told she has a shop in Little Piddle,' said the other rider, bringing his horse into step with his mate's.

'I'm not a local,' I said.

'Oh?'

'I'm staying with my nan. Back there,' I added. These big men on their high horses made me nervous.

'And you're here for what purpose today?'

'I'm just taking my cat for a walk.'

He laughed at this. Looked down at Sly, who was walking with us, but well away from the horses' big cloppitty hooves.

'Where d'you live when not at your nan's?' he asked.

'Er... Yarmouth?'

It was the first place that came to mind. I didn't

want to tell them anything I didn't have to, about myself or anything else.

'See any action there?'

'Action?'

'Fighting. In Yarmouth.'

'No.'

I didn't know if there'd been any fighting in Yarmouth – I'd never been there – but neither of the men commented, so maybe they didn't know either.

Frankie's cart was parked outside one of the first Little Piddle cottages. He was talking to an old couple by the gate. I don't think he saw me on the back of the horse, but he couldn't miss the troopers and he rushed inside with the couple, who slammed the door. There were a few others in the street today, and they also skipped indoors when they saw the troopers. The Royalists might have lost the war, but folk around here still didn't trust them or want anything to do with them.

One who actually came *out* when she saw us was Dolly Byrd. This time she didn't throw a bowl of widdle down first, which was a relief for me if not her. Probably quite a good thing for the Cavaliers too.

'Jidgey O'Dear?' she said.

'That's me,' I replied.

She hadn't said my name because she remembered it. What her 'Jidgey O'Dear' meant was 'What are you doing riding with *them*?'

'They're looking for the lacemaker,' I explained, even though she hadn't put the question into words.

'D'you know where we might find her?' asked the trooper I was riding behind.

Dolly took in the faded frills and feathers, the tangled ringlets, then thumbed the fork to the left of the dried-up river.

'Small shop with black window frames just past the Piddler's Rest.'

'The Piddler's Rest?'

'The tavern.'

'Thank you, madam, you're very kind.'

The 'madam' flustered Dolly no end, and when the trooper took off his hat and bowed to her, she actually blushed. And then we were moving again. Too soon. I hadn't got down yet.

''Scuse me,' I said, tugging at his coat.

'You still there?' he said. 'Well, I'll set you down in a tick.'

When we got to the lacemaker's I slipped down from the horse – just missing Sly, who now that we'd arrived had found the nerve to come closer to the big critter than was healthy for such a small one.

The troopers dismounted too, and strode to the shop. Men in boots like theirs had to stride. You couldn't mince in such boots. There was someone outside, sweeping the ground with a broom made of long twigs. Someone I wouldn't have been sorry not to see again before my ninety-first birthday sing-along. Fanny Nutter. I was about to beat it when I saw Dolly coming after me, so I waited.

'*And?*' she said when she reached me.

'They kidnapped me.'

'They what?'

'Gave me a lift.'

'We don't accept lifts from Royalists in Little Piddle,' she said.

'I wasn't in Little Piddle at the time, I was at the crossroads.'

'We don't accept lifts from their kind, period.'

'I didn't have any say in it, they're bigger than me. What's Miss Nutter doing at the lacemaker's?'

'Miss Nutter *is* the lacemaker.'

'What do you mean Miss Nutter is the lacemaker?'

'I mean Miss Nutter's the lacemaker.'

'Her? *She* makes *lace*?'

I stared at Miss N, who'd stopped sweeping and was chatting to the troopers like a normal person instead of the screeching old bat I'd seen at the pond.

'She does,' Dolly said. 'Quite a reputation for it too. Merchants come by all the time to buy Nutter lace.'

'Royalist soldiers too?'

'First I've seen for months. Surprised they have the nerve to show their faces here, or those uniforms.'

'Miss Nutter's going inside,' I said.

We hung about to see what the troopers would do next, but they just stood there until the lady came back out with some samples.

'They'll be wanting new collars and cuffs,' Dolly whispered. 'Cavaliers hate to look tatty.'

We snuck closer to try and hear what was said. Sly snuck with us.

'Do you know this cat?' Dolly asked.

'He's my nan's.'

'You brought him all the way from Great Piddle?'

'He followed me.'

Ever since he'd caught up with me in the field, Sly had been like a standard domestic moggy, not all stand-offish and snarly like he usually was, but as we drew near the shop his fur rose and he held back. The troopers were running the lace samples through their fingers, holding them up to the light and all, and Miss Nutter was talking about quality and prices and they were going 'Mmm' and 'Oh?' and 'Aaah,' when Sly suddenly flew at Miss N. Her hands went up, the lace she was holding flew skyward, and Sly's teeth gripped the hem of her skirt. The troopers stepped smartly back and stared as he tugged the hem like he wanted to fang it to shreds.

'He doesn't seem to like her very much,' said Dolly.

'He doesn't take to everyone,' I said.

Fanny had grabbed her broom and was trying to

beat Sly off with it, screaming in the same screechy way she'd yelled at me the day before, but he didn't let go, and when he leapt back there was an almighty rip and then he was rolling over and over inside half the skirt and Miss Nutter was standing there in long bloomers. Lace ones.

That's when I saw the funny side and started laughing fit to burst. Miss Nutter turned on me.

'Is that your cat?' she shrieked.

I was chortling too hard to speak, so Dolly answered for me.

'It's his nan's.'

'Oh! Is it now! Well, seeing as he's so entertained by the creature's performance, perhaps he would like to *emulate* it!'

I peered at her through tears of joy, but when I glimpsed the darkness of her eyes the tears dried. I stopped laughing.

And fell to my knees.

Oh, not again, I thought. But no, it wasn't a repeat of yesterday's falling-every-few-yards deal. It was something else. Something very different. I stayed on my knees. And my hands. Trotted on them towards the troopers, who were chuckling as Sly savaged his half of Miss Nutter's skirt. Then I was winding myself around their legs and licking their big boots. Yes, licking Royalist boots.

And purring.

I wasn't the only one who was not amused that I had to behave like a cat. The Cavaliers whose boots I was smooching weren't laughing now either.

'What are you doing, boy? Get off.'

'Puritan whelp. He's making fun of us.'

'I knew we shouldn't have come this far into their territory.'

'It was you who wanted the lace.'

'You too, as I recall. Away with you, brat!'

Kicked by thumping great Royalist boots, I tumbled sideways, no longer purring.

'Leave! All of you! Now!'

This was Miss Nutter, frantically covering her bloomers with her lace samples.

'You don't mean us,' one of the soldiers said to her.

'I said *all* of you!' she shouted, face like ancient thunder. 'All!'

'But we haven't decided on the lace yet.'

'Well you've missed your chance! The shop is now shut!'

She went inside and slammed the door. The troopers looked at one another, not happily. But then they shrugged, hauled themselves up into their saddles, and trotted away, grumbling quietly.

Desperate for human legs to rub against, I turned to Dolly Byrd's.

'Don't even think about it,' she said, jumping away.

'Hey, come on, I've got to,' I said. 'She's bewitched me again.'

'What was that?' a voice said. 'Did you say bewitched?'

Matthew Hopkins. With so much going on I hadn't noticed him and his assistant approaching with their witch cart.

'Miss Nutter made me act like a cat,' I said, glancing to where Sly was last time I looked. The bit of skirt was still where he'd been playing with it, but he wasn't. Maybe I did a better cat than him and he'd gone off in a strop.

'Miss Nutter?' Master Hopkins asked.

I pointed a paw at her shop. 'The lacemaker.'

'You're saying she's a witch?' he asked with a sharp jerk of the head.

I crawled to him on my hands and knees. 'What I'm saying is that thanks to her I can't stop doing stuff like this.'

I nuzzled his ankles.

'Turning people into cats,' he said, patting my head. 'New one on me.'

'Pretty new on me too,' I mewed.

'What's your name, lad?'

'My name? It's Jidgey. '

I needn't have bothered, for just then he had one of his coughing fits, which must have put a serious dent in his hearing ability because when he'd got over it he said, 'Well, Jiggy, only a witch' – his head jerked – 'could make someone behave like a cat, and she'll not get away with it!'

He stalked to the shop and tried the handle. The door was locked. He banged on the wood and shouted for Miss Nutter to come out and face Parliament's representative.

'Who's he?' Dolly asked.

'A witchfinder.'

'A witchfinder? And you shopped Fanny to him?'

'I didn't shop her, I told the truth. That she put a cat spell on me.'

'Well, he's missed her anyway. I just heard her back door slam. Probably gone to the pond for another stab at summoning the demon.'

'Nutter by name, nutter by nature,' I said, and padded on my hands and knees to the cartload of accused witches.

Master Hopkins's assistant stood by the cart. She didn't seem bothered by me standing up on my hind legs to look in, but I didn't want her hearing what I said to Nan, so I kept the O'Dear voice down.

'Nan,' I whispered. 'Miss Nutter did the eye trick again. Made me act like a cat this time.'

Nan didn't reply, probably because of the gag over her mouth. While she carried on not replying Frankie Merk rattled up with his handcart.

'What's all this?' he asked, seeing Nan chained and gagged.

'Master Hopkins accused Nan of being a witch,' I told him.

'A witch? Your nan?'

'What do you want here, man?'

The Witchfinder General was approaching.

'What I want,' Frankie said to him, 'is to know what you think you're playing at, chaining my friend up.'

'She's awaiting trial,' said Master Hopkins.

'Trial? As a witch?'

'What else? Seeking out and trying witches' – jerk – 'is what I do. The accused seems to be out,' he said to me.

'I reckon she's at Piddle Pond,' said Dolly, joining us at the cart.

'Piddle Pond?' he said. 'That's where I'm headed. Which way is it from here?'

'I'll take you.'

I stared at her. She'd offered to take him to the very pond he planned to drop my nan in. I glanced helplessly at Nan. Her eyes met mine, and when they did, I couldn't look away. But then she blinked, and I blinked too, and shook myself, stood up straight. I was no longer a cat-boy.

Master Hopkins had missed the eye-contact scene, but he did notice that I was no longer rolling about.

'Has it worn off?' he asked.

'Seems to have done.'

'Short-term spell. But the accusation's been made. You've called her a witch' – jerk – 'and she must be apprehended and tried. Show me to the pond, child,' he said to Dolly.

Dolly drew herself up haughtily. 'I'm not a child,' she said.

Master Hopkins touched the brim of his hat. 'My apologies. Lead the way please.'

'Why don't we wait here for Miss Nutter to come back?' I suggested.

He frowned at me. 'I'm a busy chap. I don't have time to waste waiting for witches' – jerk – 'to return at their leisure. Let's go.'

Dolly set off. The witchfinder walked some yards behind her with his assistant and the cartload of ladies accused of witchcraft. Frankie followed them with his handcart, which still carried Eebay Tatt's chair. There was someone else too, behind Frankie. The burly fellow no one knew. The one who'd hauled Nan out of her cottage.

'You should be a tour guide,' I said, falling in with Dolly up the front.

'I don't like witchfinders,' she said.

'So why help this one?'

'I want to see what Fanny will do to him when he confronts her.'

'She might not do anything. Might not be able to. He doesn't seem to be the sort that people get the better of. Besides, the pond's the last place I want him to go to right now.'

'Why's that?'

'He plans to chuck the accused witches in it and my nan's one of them.'

'Your nan?'

I thumbed the cart rattling along behind us. 'The one with the gag.'

'Your nan's a witch?'

'No, course she isn't, but he's made up his mind that she is and he wants to see if she can swim. And if she can't...'

'You might have mentioned this before,' Dolly said.

'I didn't get a chance.'

'No. Too busy playing cats.'

'I couldn't help that.'

'Hm!' she said, and stormed on ahead.

The horse and cart would never have made it

along the footpath I'd seen Piddle Pond from yesterday, but there was another way, a wider track, and when we were some way along it I dropped back for a word with Master Hopkins, thinking that if I could seem to be on his side, maybe I could get him to let Nan off.

'Must be exciting, job like yours,' I said.

'I don't do it for the excitement,' he grunted. 'I do it because witches' – he jerked his head sideways – 'cannot be permitted to walk the earth.'

'Can they run?' I asked.

He frowned. 'I beg your pardon?'

'Joke.'

His frown became a scowl. 'I don't approve of jokes.'

'Oh. Really. I'll try and remember that. Sir, I was wondering.'

'Wondering?'

'If there's any way you can tell if a person's a witch without putting them in water.'

'Why do you want to know?'

'Well, this witchfinding business is new to me, and there's so much I want to learn, and...well, I never met anyone like you before.'

His scowl smoothed out. 'It's very refreshing to hear such words from one so young. So you're keen to learn more, are you?'

'Keen? I'm chin-to-toe fascinated by the whole kafloozle. I want to know everything, so that when I grow up I can be just like you.'

He bared his teeth, which were yellow. 'Your name. Jiggy, wasn't it?'

'Jiggy? No, it...' I stopped. What did I care what he called me? 'Yeah, Jiggy, that's me.'

'What was the question again, Jiggy?'

'Question?'

'The one about telling if a person's a witch,' he said, jerking wildly.

'Oh, yes. Can you can tell if they're a witch without dunking them?'

'Well, my spellchecker's a good pointer,' he said.

'Your what?'

He raised the walking stick with the silver handle. 'It has properties that can identify the presence of dark magic. I thump the ground between myself and a suspect and if it trembles I know that she or he is a witch.' (Jerk.)

'And it always works?'

'Every time.'

'Some stick,' I said.

When we reached Piddle Pond, Dolly pointed out Miss Nutter, fifty or so yards along the bank, arms stretched towards the water, chanting quietly. I'm glad to say that between rushing into her shop in a fury and rushing out the back door (probably in another fury) she'd managed to cover her bloomers with some more material.

'What's she doing?' Master Hopkins asked.

'Trying to summon the demon of the pond,' Dolly told him.

'Demon?'

'Her sister, who was burned as a witch—'

'She was?'

'—claimed to have summoned him and he's thought to have been in the pond ever since. Fanny wants to call him up and use him to get back at a few people. I don't personally think there's anything down there except mud, fish and weeds, but then I don't believe all that witch malarkey either.'

Master Hopkins scowled. 'Such talk comes close to blasphemy, girl.'

'Some other talk comes close to tosh – *man,'* Dolly replied.

The Witchfinder General told his assistant to mind the prisoners, then set off along the bank. The burly man who'd bundled Nan into the cart back at the village green went after him, like a big shadow. When Master Hopkins shouted 'You – woman!' at Miss Nutter, she stopped chanting, lowered her arms, and waited for him and the other man to approach.

'Here's your chance,' Dolly said to me.

'What for?' I asked.

'To free your nan.'

'What about the assistant?'

'Bribe her.'

'If you mean with money I haven't got any.'

'Talk to her nicely then.'

Frankie was already tugging at Nan's chains. The assistant leant on the side of the cart, watching him struggle.

'They're padlocked,' she said.

'Where are the keys?' Frankie asked her.

'Boss has 'em.'

'So that's that,' I said.

There was an 'Mmmm-mmmm' sound from Nan, wriggling about as much as she could in her chains. Frankie tugged her gag down.

'Took you long enough to do that!' Nan said.

'I was more concerned with getting you out of there,' Frankie said.

'Well do that. I don't care how, just do it.'

'We don't have the keys.'

'I know you don't have the keys, but there must be another way.'

'Witchcraft, anyone?' I said hopefully to the others in the cart.

'If we had, don't you think we'd have used it by now?' one of them said.

'Interesting scene about to occur down there,' said Dolly.

All eyes followed her finger (to where it pointed, I mean). Master Hopkins stood in front of Miss Nutter while the burly man stood a few feet behind her with his back to the water. At first Miss Nutter looked like she was wondering what was going on, but then the truth seemed to dawn and she turned and looked the big man in the eye. When she did this he went all rigid, like a poker had been shoved up him – and stayed that way, as if turned to stone. When Miss N turned back to Hopkins, he thumped his stick on the ground and it started shaking.

'He used that on me,' said one of the women in the cart.

'And me,' said another.

'Me too,' said the third.

'What does it do?' Dolly asked.

'If it shakes,' I explained, 'it means the person he's standing in front of is a witch.'

'It means nothing of the kind,' one of the carted women snorted. 'It's just a stick he uses to con people that a person is one.'

'That's what I meant,' I said.

'Witch! Witch! Witch!'

This was Master Hopkins shouting at Miss Nutter, head jerking sideways each time he said the word. And what did Miss N do? She snatched the stick from him and brought it down across her knee.

Hopkins stared at her. 'What are you doing?'

'What does it look like?' she said.

'Mr Sweetman, stop her!' he shouted at the fellow behind her.

But Mr Sweetman didn't stop her. He didn't move a muscle. He just stood there while Fanny carried on trying to break the spellchecker over her bony knee. Master Hopkins only tried to stop her once himself, but she whacked his shoulder and he didn't try again. It took six attempts to snap the stick, and when it was done Miss Nutter lobbed both bits far out into the pond.

'My spellchecker!' Master Hopkins howled.

'And now for you two,' said Miss Nutter.

She flicked the chest of still-as-a-statue Mr Sweetman, who instantly turned about and walked into the pond, very stiffly, like a big toy soldier. He kept going as the water rose to his knees, then his waist, his chest.

'Mr Sweetman, get back here!' screamed the Witchfinder General.

But Mr Sweetman kept right on, and the water reached his neck, then his mouth, his hairline, and finally covered his head. After that he was just bubbles, and then the bubbles stopped, and that was the last anyone saw of him.

Now, drawing herself up to her full height, which was a fair bit taller than her accuser, Miss

Nutter said: 'And what shall we do with *you*, witchfinder?'

Master Hopkins stepped back in haste – too much haste, because he tripped over his feet and sat down sharply. Miss Nutter leaned towards him, but he scurried away on his bum until he was far enough from her to jump to his feet and scamper off.

'He got off lightly,' sighed Nan with regret.

'More lightly than the other chap,' said Frankie.

'I wouldn't go shedding any tears for that one,' said she. 'He was Hopkins's lackey. Hopkins himself is the one she should've seen to. He's a menace. Disposed of more hapless innocents than all the other witchfinders put together, he has. I've heard it said that he recently hanged sixteen accused of witchcraft in a single day.'

The colour drained from Frankie's cheeks. 'Sixteen?'

'Sixteen. We four will be far less than a good day's work for him.' She raised her voice as Hopkins drew near. 'Mad Fanny too much for you, eh, witchfinder?'

He tossed his ring of keys to his assistant.

'Bridget! Unfasten one of those chains!'

'What about her?' Bridget asked, nodding towards Miss Nutter, who'd gone back to chanting at the water like nothing had happened.

'She'll keep. Release one of the suspects. We're starting the trials!'

While Bridget undid one of the padlocks, her boss lifted the chair down from their cart. The chair had leather straps, and there was a wooden board with four wheels fixed to its feet. He carried the chair to the water's edge.

'A chair with wheels?' I said, going after him.

'My dunking chair,' he snapped. He didn't seem in a great mood for some reason.

'Yes,' I said. 'But wheels?'

'So we can push the accused into the water,' he said. 'Wheel 'em in, give 'em a chance to prove their innocence by drowning, then wheel 'em back. The old method is very primitive by comparison.'

'What was the old method?'

'We just tied their thumbs and toes together and chucked 'em in.' He relaxed a bit. Stroked his chair with pride. 'My personal invention. Quite a technological advance, I feel.'

'Someone should give you a business innovation award,' I said.

He seemed to like that. 'You know,' he said, 'you remind me of myself when I was a lad.'

'I do? Well...thanks.'

'Jiggy, how would you feel about joining me?'

'Joining you?'

'I'm short of an assistant right now. If you don't mind sleeping rough, eating badly, and lynching people – burning them on cold days – the job's yours.'

'Gosh,' I said. 'That is so tempting.'

'I'm not a witch, I'm not a witch! I never did nobody no 'arm!'

The woman Bridget had released was squealing like pins had been stuck into her. She was a big lady, wobbly in almost every place, but sort of timid-looking. Big as she was, she was no match for Bridget, who forced her into the wheeled chair and buckled the straps around her.

'You set that woman free, Hopkins, you devil!' bawled my nan from the cart.

He laughed. '*Me* a devil? It's her and her kind that have the devil in them. In a minute we'll find out if he'll bear her up. Then we'll see if he'll save you.'

I went back to the cart. 'How are we going to get Nan out of this?' I said to Frankie.

'No idea,' he said.

'Well, if you do get one, you might like to include us in the big escape plan,' one of the women said gruffly.

'Why does he think you're a witch anyway?' I asked her.

'Eustace Pratt,' she said.

'Useless prat?'

'Eustace. Pratt. My next-door neighbour. We been thorns in one another's sides for years, and when he heard the Witchfinder General was in the vicinity, Pratt told him I'd called up the storm that whipped the new thatch off his roof. Bad thatch job is what that was, cheap foreign labour, but all it takes is one person to accuse another of being a witch and next thing you know the accused is hauled off for trial and most times out of ten that's it.'

'I wonder what Hopkins gets out of it?' mused Dolly Byrd.

'He's paid on results,' said Nan. 'From what I hear he gets more for every conviction than most working men earn in a month.'

'The more the merrier for him then,' said Frankie.

'Who pays him?' I asked Nan.

'Sometimes the accuser, sometimes a town council, whoever wants rid of someone and is prepared to cough up his fee.'

'No one paid him to get rid of you.'

'No. He's probably doing me for free, just because I stood up to—'

She was interrupted by a shriek from the big woman in the dunking chair, which Bridget was wheeling into the shallows.

'I'm innocent! I never done no magic, I wouldn't know 'ow!'

'Now where have I heard *that* before?' said Master Hopkins.

Bridget pushed the chair further and further in. The woman cried and shouted all the way. When the water covered her lap, Master H said, 'Now!' Bridget tipped the chair forward and the woman went under, and all that the rest of us could do was wait until Bridget was told to bring the chair up again. The woman was gasping but still alive.

'Proof!' Master Hopkins cried. 'The Devil has born her up! She's officially a witch!' He twitched triumphantly.

'She wasn't under long enough to drown,' Frankie said.

'He didn't want her to,' said Nan.

'Well, he's not all bad then,' said I.

She looked at me sadly. 'Jidgey. Think about it.'

I thought about it. 'Oh, you mean he *wants* her to be a witch.'

'Exactly. That way he can hang her, and be paid by her accusers.'

'Someone should ask him why a devil that saves his servants from drowning doesn't also set them free,' said Frankie.

'Someone could also ask him,' said Dolly, 'why the Devil doesn't knock him into the next county, or worse.'

Bridget had almost finished unstrapping the large woman when one of the chair's legs gave way and it lurched sideways, taking her with it.

'You've cursed my chair, witch!' Master Hopkins roared with a mighty jerk.

'She was too heavy for your damned chair, you twerp!' Nan shouted.

Bridget pulled the woman to her feet, hauled her back to the cart, and chained her up again.

'Broken beyond repair!' Master Hopkins wailed, inspecting the chair's shattered leg. 'Now what will we do?'

'How about we all go and share a nice pot of tea?' Frankie suggested.

The sound of his voice reminded Master Hopkins that he wasn't the only one with a chair.

'You. Fellow. Bring me your chair.'

'My chair?' said Frankie.

'The one in your cart.'

'You can't have that, it's for my customers.'

'It was. It's not now. I'm commandeering it in the name of Parliament.'

'Don't you give it him, Frankie,' said Nan.

'He'll do as he's told or swim with you,' Master Hopkins barked.

'You'd have to accuse him of being a witch to do that,' said she.

He scowled meanly. 'And don't think I wouldn't.'

'I got to give it him, Kat,' Frankie said apologetically.

As he took the chair down I heard a sharp intake of breath. So did Dolly Byrd, who was standing next to me.

'What's up?' she asked me.

'Nothing. Just sharply intaking some breath.'

I'd had an idea. A breathtaking one. A plan that might, just might, save my nan.

Hopkins carried Frankie's chair to the pond and knelt down to attach the wheeled board to its legs. He didn't seem to have much idea how to do it. I strolled to him.

'Problem?' I said.

He glanced at me. 'People usually do manual jobs for me.'

'I'll give it a go if you like.'

'Oh, how kind.'

I knew I could do it. I'm good with my hands. Don't know who I get it from. Not my dad, that's for sure. Dad's useless at everything, Mum says. That's why she went to war with him. Said someone had to look after him. She was probably his human shield.

Master Hopkins watched me work for a while, then said: 'Could you build a scaffold, Jiggy?'

'Scaffold?'

'To hang witches from.' (Jerk.) 'I've got a folding one in the cart, but it's getting rather rickety from over-use.'

'Bit short notice,' I said.

'I don't mean now. I'll make do with the one I've got today. But would you be able to make one, given time?'

I said that I reckoned I could build him a pretty neat scaffold. I didn't actually plan to do it, of course. I was just trying to keep in his good books.

'This is yours if those wheels are firm,' he said, flashing a coin at me. 'And there'll be more than one for a decent flat-pack scaffold.'

'I don't get to see many of those,' I said, eyeing the coin.

'There's no shortage of them in my line. There are more witches' – jerk – 'in this part of the world than you can shake a stick at.'

'Or a spellchecker?' I said brightly.

He frowned. 'Is that another joke?'

I straightened my face. 'Sorry.'

He turned away and gazed across the pond to where the two parts of his stick went down. 'I'll be lost without my spellchecker,' he murmured.

'What about your man?'

'My man?'

'The one who walked into the water. Lost without him too?'

'Oh, Mr Sweetman.' He shrugged. 'As with coins, there's no shortage of types like him. Spellcheckers, though, that's something else again.'

'You can't get another?'

'I believe mine was unique,' he said sadly.

'Where'd you get it?'

'Bess Clarke of Manningtree. Manningtree's where I live. Widow Clarke was my first witch.' He jerked his head. 'A rattle-boned old biddy with one leg. I removed it from her.'

'Her leg?'

'The spellchecker.'

'Oh, you nicked it.'

He scowled. 'You can't nick from a witch! Witches are the Devil's spawn. Once convicted, they surrender all rights to property and possessions.'

'What was she doing with a spellchecker?'

I asked. 'I mean if she was a witch, why would she want to discover other witches? Short of witchy pals or something?'

'She cast spells with it. Inflicted pain and sickness on those she fell out of favour with. As a non-witch' – jerk – 'I can't do such things, and nor would I want to. In my hands, the spellchecker could only be used to identify those who *make* spells.'

'There,' I said. 'Done.'

I stood up and pushed the chair back and forth a few times. It worked a treat. Master Hopkins slipped the promised coin into my pocket, then transferred the straps from the broken chair to Frankie's.

'Bridget,' he said. 'Bring that hag here.'

'Which one?'

'The latest one. The troublesome one.'

Bridget unlocked Nan's padlock and unchained her. Nan put up quite a fight as Bridget hauled her across to the chair. I wanted to go to her and tell her not to worry, that everything would be all right, but I couldn't with Bridget and Hopkins so close. I glanced at Frankie. He looked so distressed, like he was going to burst into tears. I thought of taking him aside and telling him of my plan. I might have too if he hadn't suddenly turned on his heel and walked away fast, like he couldn't face what was going to happen to Nan.

So it was just me. Me and a plan that might not work. If it didn't, Nan would either drown or…

I shuddered. Couldn't bear to think of it.

CHAPTER EIGHT

Nan was still kicking up a fuss when Bridget started buckling her into the chair. Time for me to step in. Start the plan.

'Keep still, woman!' I said sternly.

Nan froze. Stared at me. Which allowed Bridget to finish strapping her in. 'Jidgey? Why are you aiding this brute?'

'I'm just being helpful,' I said, like it was the right thing to do.

'You know this woman?' Master Hopkins asked me.

'I've seen her about, is all.'

'She called you Jidgey.'

'Yeah, she doesn't even know my proper name.'

'So it seems. Bridget. Wheel her in.'

Bridget started to do this, but I jumped in front of the chair before it reached the water.

'Can I do it?'

'You?' Master Hopkins said.

'Yes, why not? Got to start somewhere if I'm going to join you.'

'Oh, so you accept my offer?'

I grinned happily. 'Best I've had all year.'

He clapped me on the shoulder. 'I commend your enthusiasm, lad. You'll make a fine witchfinder.' (Jerk.) 'Go to it, my boy!'

Bridget looked a bit put out when I took over the chair. 'I enjoy this bit,' she said.

'You can do the next one,' I said, pushing the chair into the shallows.

Nan looked up at me as we bumped over the stones.

'I can't believe you're doing this,' she said.

I leant down and whispered: 'I'm trying to save you.'

'Save me? How will tipping me face down in the water save me?'

'You've got to do two things. First, when I give the word, take a deep breath – I mean *deep* breath – and hold it. Then, when you're under the water, you must shake your whole body like a lunatic.'

'What will that achieve?'

'Just do it, Nan – please? Wriggle like you're in a real panic.'

'I will be.'

'Great.'

'We don't chat with the accused, Jiggy, we swim them!' Master Hopkins said. 'Then it's up to their maker or the Devil, whichever's their master.'

When the water covered Nan's lap, I said to her, very softly, out of the side of my mouth, 'Trust me, Nan. Huge breath now, and once the water covers you, wriggle like crazy and don't stop.'

She took the huge breath, I tipped the chair forward, and even before she was under she started wriggling like a madwoman.

'Come on, come on,' I said to myself, giving the chair an extra shake as the back of Nan's dress filled and bubbled up with water.

'That'll do, Jiggy,' said Master Hopkins after about twenty seconds. 'Raise the chair. Let's see if the Devil's saved her.'

'She's still wriggling,' I said. 'Better give her a bit longer.'

'I said now!' he shrieked in a surprisingly high-pitched voice.

Of course, I thought. He wants to see her on the end of a rope. But not for money this time. He just doesn't like her.

I glanced his way. 'Bringing her up,' I said miserably.

My plan had failed. The chair that had kicked me into the field behind Nan's cottage hadn't sent her anywhere. Maybe she hadn't wriggled enough. Maybe the weight of the water had slowed her wriggle too much. I didn't know. I sighed. Turned back to pull the chair up, and found it quite a bit lighter than before. Then I saw why.

It was empty. Nanless.

'Hey!' I cried.

It was a shout of triumph, but it could have been taken for one of shock.

Master Hopkins charged to the water's edge. 'Where is she?'

I dragged the empty chair to the bank. 'She must have wriggled out of the straps,' I said.

'She can't have!' said Bridget, snatching up the broken leg of the first chair and running into the water. 'They were tight! I made sure of it!'

She started thrashing the water with the chair

leg. She thrashed and thrashed it, then dipped her head in to look beneath the surface.

'No sign of her!' she said, coming up, head dripping.

'Where can she have got to?' I wondered innocently.

'The Devil's taken her!' Master Hopkins said. 'She must have been one of his dearest helpmates!'

'Yeah, that must be it,' I said, unbuckling the chair's straps to give me a reason to turn away and hide my smile.

Bridget stomped out of the water, threw the piece of wood aside, and scratched an armpit. 'That's what happens when you give a job to an amateur!' she snarled at me.

The smile was still on my face when I realised something I should have thought of before I tipped Nan in the water. That although I might have saved her from a hanging, I might not have saved her from a drowning. I'd expected Mr Tatt's chair to fling her out, straps or no straps, but Piddle Pond was not small. It was a pond of some size. So who was to say that the chair hadn't lobbed her into another part of it rather than far away, onto dry land? If Nan had ended up in a deeper part of the pond when that big breath of hers was all gone, she'd have gulped water and snuffed it. How would I explain that to my mother when she eventually came for me? 'Mum, I pushed Nan into the pond and forced her under, and she sort of drowned, sorry 'bout that, what's for tea?'

I was thinking all this when I caught a movement across the water, in a thicket on the opposite bank. Someone dodging between the trunks.

Nan!

She was safe!

I went to Dolly Byrd. 'Listen,' I said. 'My nan's in those trees over there. Do me a favour. Go and tell her to stay put for a while.'

Dolly peered across the water. 'Your nan's over there?'

'Yes.'

'But...how?'

'Tell you later. Don't let them see where you're going.'

She could have asked more questions, but to her credit she didn't. She backed slowly away, trying to look like slow backing was her normal way of walking. Master Hopkins wasn't interested in her anyway. He was still gazing at the water, muttering stuff about sorcery and devils. Then he started to cough – badly. 'She's cast an evil spell on me,' he said, coughing like his insides were about to jerk up his throat and trickle out of his mouth.

'You had that cough before you met her,' Bridget said sourly, scratching a hip.

'Well she's made it worse!'

He groped behind him for something to sit on till he stopped coughing and found Mr Tatt's chair. The seat was wet, but he was coughing so hard that he probably didn't notice.

Just then I heard a loud buzzing sound. I glanced towards it. A bee. But not a lone bee. Hard on the wings of bee one were dozens more. I ducked, the way you do when bees are near, but they buzzed on by, and in seconds were hovering around Master Hopkins in the chair. At first he was coughing so furiously that he had his eyes tight shut and didn't see them, but then one of them landed on his cheek and the eye above it half opened and looked down at it. Then the second eye opened, and the pair of them wandered this way and that and took in the other bees buzzing around him like he was their personal honeypot. Seeing how many there were somehow put an end to his coughing and once he was still, some of the bees landed on his shoulders, some on his collar, some on his hat. Only when a couple more joined the one on his cheek did Hopkins get active again, batting the bees away and jerking around to avoid the ones that hadn't settled yet. But bees don't buzz off just because you don't seem terrifically fond of them. The more frantic you get, the keener they are to be near you, and when more of them land on you, you get even more frantic, which makes them a tad tetchy.

Which is what happened now.

Soon, Master Hopkins's head could hardly be seen for bees. They weren't stinging, just badgering him (or beeing him), which made him wriggle quite a bit more than Nan had under the water. More even than I had the two times the chair tossed me into the field. And suddenly...

The chair was empty!

And way out in the middle of the pond, Master Hopkins was splashing and thrashing frantically.

'How'd he do that?' said a voice behind me.

It was Frankie Merk, ducking the bees that were now swarming to the person with him. His cousin, Widow Atterbury.

'Oh, they're *your* bees,' I said to her.

She gave me one of those big wrinkly smiles of hers. 'Frankie thought they might come in handy here. Job done, my honeys,' she said to the bees. 'Home with you now!'

And off they went, in a single tight swarm, back to their hives.

'I thought you'd run out on us,' I said to Frankie.

He hoisted a bulging bag that hadn't been on his shoulder earlier. 'Me, run out on your nan? Never!'

'She could've drowned while you were away.'

'I was as quick as I could be,' he said. 'But she got away anyway, it seems.'

He was looking past me. I turned and saw Dolly Byrd and Nan strolling towards us, round the bank.

'Smart woman, my Kat. Lucky one too, grandson like you.'

'Me?' I said. 'I did nothing.'

I couldn't admit it. No one knew what the chair

could do. Just me. And Nan, now. But there was a look in Frankie's eye that said he knew more than he was letting on.

'You're a good lad, Jiggy,' he said.

'Jidgey,' I corrected.

'Oh,' he said, 'I think you got yourself a new name today.'

I thought about that. Jiggy. Well, why not? At least it wasn't the name of a dead nun.

'Where did she come from?' Bridget said, noticing Nan approaching with Dolly.

'My guess is the other side of the pond,' I said.

'But it's way over there!'

'She's a good swimmer.'

'Well, *he* isn't,' she said, scratching her bottom. She meant Master Hopkins, who was splashing about insanely. 'When he hired me he said he hoped no one ever accused him of witchcraft because he'd be proved innocent without any trouble.'

'He told me he doesn't like jokes,' I said.

'Whether he does or he doesn't, he's not laughing now,' said Nan, joining us, linking my arm, and giving me a big wet kiss on the cheek.

'Fanny's off,' said Dolly.

Miss Nutter was stalking away in what looked like a huff.

'Probably had it with all the commotion,' I said.

Miss Nutter was barely out of the picture when something happened in the pond. Right about where Master Hopkins was splashing so desperately, the water began to churn like it was being whisked by a giant hand, and then part of it rose up in the shape of an enormous head – not a very pretty head – with Master H on top of it like a human hat.

'So there *is* a demon,' Dolly gasped in wonder.

'All Fanny's efforts and she missed it,' said Nan.

'It can't stay,' said Widow Atterbury.

Nan agreed with her. 'No, it can't. We don't want no demons in the Piddles. Witchfinders is bad enough.'

'Yes, and we've had all we want of them too,' said Widow Atterbury.

She and Nan nodded at one another and walked to the bank where, standing side by side, one tall and thin, one short and dumpy, they stretched their arms out over the water. When they did that, the demon's watery mane flew out in long tangled sprays and he turned towards them like he suspected something was about to occur. His eyes were yellow. Then Nan and Widow Atterbury began chanting a rhyme that they hadn't had time to rehearse yet spoke as one.

'O demon of the Piddle's pond
Pay no heed to Fanny's wand
But harken to this wiccan pair
Listen well and take good care
Go below and stay quite still
Stay there from today until
A thousand piddles plus just one
In Piddle Pond are someday done
Only then may you arise
In whatever fine disguise
Now conjured pond life, go below –
Go you, demon, GO, GO, GO!'

Until they shouted the last line, the creature in the pond just glared at them, mouth moving silently like he wanted to gobble them up but was held back by some invisible force. While he fumed and the waters churned, Master Hopkins spluttered and thrashed about on the demon's head like he was trying to get the hang of the backstroke. But when the two ladies bawled 'GO, GO, GO!' the monster's hair shivered and coiled like a dozen strangled water snakes, and he jerked his great wet head so sharply that Master Hopkins went flying. Then the demon's mouth opened in soundless rage, and down he plunged, back into the depths from which he'd come.

In a minute or less the water was still again, except where Master Hopkins lay in the weeds of the near bank, coughing and gasping for air. Nan and Widow Atterbury turned from the pond looking rather pleased with themselves.

'So you *are* a witch!' I said to Nan. 'You *both* are!'

'Only when the need arises,' Nan replied. 'We prefer to keep what might be called a low profile if it wasn't such a stupid expression.'

'Just make our honey and lotions and lead a quiet life,' beamed Widow Atterbury.

'And witches who lead quiet lives and keep low profiles can't save themselves from *drowning*?' I said to Nan in disbelief.

'Sadly, no,' she said. 'The ability to save lives, even our own, isn't one of our skills.'

'Are you a witch too?' I asked Frankie.

'Me?' he said. 'God forbid.' He frowned at his little cousin. 'One's quite enough for one family.'

'I'm not one either, in case you wondered,' said Dolly Byrd.

'I didn't,' I said.

'Evil-doers! Emissaries of Satan!'

This was Master Hopkins, struggling out of the

wet weeds. As he got up he was overcome by such a huge coughing fit that he almost slid back in. Frankie grabbed him by the arm, but got the big shrug-off for his trouble, and Master Hopkins carried on coughing, worse than ever, doubled over and holding his chest.

'Sounds like you could do with a good cough mixture,' Nan said. 'I got an excellent one back at the cottage. My own brew.'

'I want nothing of yours, witch!' He jerked fiercely.

'I weren't offering,' Nan said. 'Just saying I got one that I might give you if I cared what happened to you, which I don't.'

Master Hopkins turned to Bridget. 'I need...' He broke off with a splutter, took a deep ragged breath, started again. 'I need my bed.'

'Which bed?' Bridget asked, scratching her chest with both hands.

'My own. I'm sick. Need to recover before continuing my work.'

'Manningtree's a long way.'

'It is, but get me there and' – he coughed horribly – 'and I'll give you half what I've made this past fortnight.'

'Only half?'

'Very well, all! Now remove those' – he jerked in advance for a change – 'witches.'

'Suspected witches,' said Bridget, scratching her left knee. 'God, I'm so *itchy* all of a sudden!'

'A witch itch?' Frankie asked Nan on the quiet.

She shook her head. 'Not my doing. Some get it, some don't.'

'Get those wretches out of the cart and take me home!' Master Hopkins commanded Bridget.

Bridget released the three women. They climbed down wearing the first smiles I'd seen on their faces.

Taking their place in the cart, Master Hopkins said to me: 'Jiggy. Ride up here if you wish. I'll...' – *cough-cough* – '...I'll start your training when I'm better.'

'To seek out witches?' I asked.

'Naturally. Of course.'

'Thanks, but if it's all the same to you I'll stay with my nan.'

'Your nan?'

I put my arm round Nan's shoulders and saw him gape from me to her and back again. Then, slowly, he got it, and his expression changed to a greater fury than the one on the demon's face as it was forced back into the deep.

'Bridget, get me away from these...*peasants*!'

He climbed into his cart and lay down, coughing and gasping, gasping and coughing.

'Not long for this world, by the look of him,' said Widow Atterbury.

'Let's hope there's not a next one then,' said Nan. 'I wouldn't want to find him waiting there for me.'

Bridget was scratching just about all over by this time.

'Going to offer her some itchycoo cream?' Frankie asked Nan.

'Not while she's in that beast's employ,' she replied.

As we watched the madly scratching Bridget walk the horse and cart away with the Witchfinder General coughing like a maniac in the back, I thought of a couple of things that I was quite keen to get cleared up.

'That chant of yours,' I said to Nan and Widow Atterbury. 'You said "pay no heed to Fanny's wand". I didn't see Miss Nutter with a wand.'

'Have you never heard of poetic licence?' said Nan.

'And "a thousand piddles plus just one"? I didn't get that either.'

She and Widow Atterbury twinkled at one another.

'Our little joke,' said Widow A. 'Thanks to that spell the only way the demon will ever get out of the pond is if one person wees in it a thousand and one times. How likely is *that*?'

'Look, Kat, you been followed,' said Frankie suddenly.

Nan's unsociable cat had just stalked into view.

'Sly, what you doing all the way out here?' Nan said, falling to her knees beside him. When she cuddled him he didn't seem to mind one bit. If I'd made such a fuss of him he'd have had my eyes out. You probably have to be a witch.

Now Frankie opened the bag he'd brought from Honey Cottage and took out a jug of his cousin's home-made cordial, a pot of honey, a loaf of bread, and a knife.

Then, under that big blue August sky, he, Nan, Dolly Byrd, Tilly Atterbury, Sly and I – plus the three women from the cart – seated ourselves at the water's edge and ate and drank in a very cheerful sort of way.

It was a good day for a picnic by a village pond.

Jiggy O'Dear, 1647

HISTORICAL NOTES

The events in this book take place during a break in the English Civil War, which began in 1642 and ended in 1651. On one side were the Royalists (Cavaliers) and on the other the Parliamentarians (Puritans or Roundheads). Matthew Hopkins, who operated at this time, almost certainly believed himself a good person exposing evildoers. A strict religious upbringing would have left him in little doubt that servants of Satan walked the earth as witches. It became his mission to destroy them, which he did, wherever he managed to 'convict' suspects, often cheered on by enthusiastic villagers or townsfolk who turned out specially for the occasion.

For the better part of the centuries since his day, Hopkins's own fate was unknown. A popular theory had it that he himself was accused of witchcraft and disposed of in suitably nasty fashion. The irony of such an end for such a man has some appeal but the reality seems to be that he died in his bed, in Manningtree, of the lung-rattling consumption that had been plaguing him for some time, to be buried the same day – 12th August 1647 – in the graveyard of the since-demolished church of St Mary the Virgin at nearby Mistley Heath.

Jidgey. I've only come across this name once, in Cornwall, where there's a tiny hamlet called St Jidgey. Little is known about the saint herself other than that she appears to have been born in 479 or thereabouts and was one of twenty or more offspring of King Brychan Brycheiniog, who 'evangelised northern Cornwall'.

Nutter. I borrowed the name from a family of Lancashire Nutters, one of whom, Alice, a property-owning gentlewoman, was hanged as a witch on an apparently trumped-up murder charge. This was in 1612, though – long before Matthew Hopkins was born.

A descendant of Fanny Nutter – Ophelia Mooney – was to become the nemesis of Jiggy O'Dear's own descendant, Jiggy McCue. Their 21st century conflict is described in a book called *Rudie Dudie*, in which we learn of the powers of suggestion passed down to Ms Mooney by Miss Nutter.

The story of how Piddle Pond came into being over a hundred and eighty years before Jiggy O'Dear's adventure there can be read in *Jiggy's Magic Balls*, in which an earlier Jiggy (Jiggy d'Cuer) encounters two gentlemen who were to become so legendary that in our day people travel from all over the world to see where they never lived.

In the centuries after Jiggy O'Dear's time, the villages of Great Piddle and Little Piddle were gradually abandoned and the buildings crumbled into the earth or were tumbled by man. The river dried up completely, though Piddle Pond somehow retained its water and eventually became known as the Piddle Pool. By our time, no one knew that anything powerful lurked in the pool until Jiggy McCue chanced to pee in it a thousand and one times and became a certain creature's master for about three minutes. For the full story of that piddling encounter, read the Jiggy McCue book, *The Meanest Genie*.

Michael Lawrence

Jiggy's medieval life is one dirty dung heap of trouble after another. Worse, he has to work for the dumbest Knight in the land, Sir Bozo de Beurk. But when Jiggy discovers a pair of magic balls, his fortunes might be about to change...

In stores and online NOW!

'Joust Hilarious!'
The Daily Chain Mail

978 1 40830 803 5 £5.99 PB
OUT NOW!

www.jiggymccue.com

Read on for an extract of *Jiggy's Magic Balls*!

Well, here I am, up to my armpits in mud and rust, talking to myself once again. I talk to myself because mine are the only ears that listen to me. No one else's listen because I'm just another peasant kid. I'm not even a squire yet, even if I do serve a knight with a full suit of armour. My knight is Sir Bozo de Beurk, and his armour isn't much better than scrap metal, but that's not the point. A knight's a knight and armour's armour if you close your eyes. Sir Bozo isn't the brightest light in the knight sky, but at least his wife isn't about any more. His wife was called Ratface. Well, that's what I called her. Lady Ratface thought she was really something. Always trying to make out that her origins weren't almost as humble as mine. 'Ow! So-nace-to-mate-yer,' she'd coo when she was introduced to people she wanted to impress. Didn't impress me one bit. Not that she tried. Just shouted orders at me the whole time and called me names. I wasn't fond of her.

As well as a wife, Sir Bozo had a castle once. Crumbling old place, very draughty, left to him by some distant cousin who'd run out of other surviving relatives. Rubbish as it was, Bozo was quite fond of the castle, probably because he'd never had one of his own before. When Lady Ratface decided she could do better than Bozo in the knight department she hired this dodgy legal wizard, Spivvel Merlin, who had a rep for getting good deals for greedy wives. Sir Bozo wasn't hugely rich, though, so all Merlin got for Lady R was the lousy castle, which she immediately put up for sale. There were no takers, but then Merlin himself made an offer for it, and she accepted, so it was his now, which really choked Sir B because him and Merlin had been mortal enemies since they were at school together.

After the divorce, the only possessions Sir Bozo was left with were his horse, a shed on boggy ground, an allotment, and an old sword he won at school way back. The boggy shed was where we lived and the allotment was where most of our food came from. Sometimes he sent me to the nearby river to catch fish. I wasn't great at that, so fish was off the menu more often than on it. Because he missed castle life, Sir Bozo spent the last of his loot on wooden battlements for the shed and a drawbridge for the moat we didn't have. He tried to get a moat going by peeing from the battlements, and gave me instructions to do likewise. The flies were quite thick round Castle-de-Beurk-on-the-Allotment.

There wasn't a whole lot to do once I'd performed my menial duties, so it was just as well I had a hobby. I carved things out of wood. Things like back-scratchers, animals, spoons, stuff like that. The day the big something happened that was to change my life I was sitting on the drawbridge (a plank) over the piddling moat putting the finishing touches to an egg.

'You have quite a gift,' a smooth voice said.

I looked up. Spiv Merlin. I'd only seen him once before, but I'd know him anywhere because he wasn't like anyone else...

'Fang-tastically funny!'
The Garlic Press

What would you do if you were
attacked by vampires?
Edwardian butcher's son Jiggy Offal-Trype
knows what he'd do. Run.
But he can't. He has to fight back.
Luckily, he has these killer new skills...

The second HILARIOUS Jiggy's Genes book –
in stores and online NOW!

OUT NOW!

www.jiggymccue.com

Do you think you're funny?

Fancy yourself as a published author?

Send us a joke that would make Jiggy McCue laugh and it could feature in a Jiggy McCue book!

Email your joke to jiggy.jokes@jiggymccue.com or send it to us at Jiggy Jokes, Hachette Children's Books, 338 Euston Road, London NW1 3BH

Don't forget to include your name and age!

Here are some of our favourite jokes so far...

I've always had an overactive imagination. Like the time I found myself drowning in an ocean made out of Tango. It took me a while to work out it was just a Fanta-sea!

Chelsie Coghlan, 10, East Sussex

What is smelly and sounds like a bell?
DUUUUUUUUUUUNNNNNNNNGGGGGGGGGGG!!!!!!!

Hollie Robinson, 10, Hertfordshire

How do you get Pikachu on a bus?
Poke-m-on!

Caleb Andrews, 6, Bucks

What did the inflatable Headmaster say to the inflatable boy who brought a pin into the inflatable school?
'You've let the school down, you've let me down and most importantly – you've let yourself down!'

Ella Davis, 12, Surrey